THE CURSE OF THE RAVEN

Raven Son: Book Two

NICHOLAS KOTAR

WAYSTONE PRESS

THE CURSE OF THE RAVEN

(Raven Son: Book Two)

Copyright © Nicholas Kotar 2017

Cover Design by Books Covered Ltd.

Published by Waystone Press 2017

ISBN: 9780998847924

LCCN: 2017913721

❀ Created with Vellum

To Adrian and Emilia

In the year of the Covenant 1066, the great city of Vasyllia, the very heart of the known world, was betrayed to an invading army of nomad Gumiren by its own people. What many did not know, but suspected, was that the invading southerners were no more than a tool in the hand of Vasyllia's ancient enemy. He has many names, that demon. The Raven. The Great Changer. The Bringer of Darkness. But as often happens, in the moment of the Raven's ascendance was the seed of his demise planted. All that remained was for at least a few Vasylli to remain true to the Old Ways until the time of reclamation. But when the Healer returns, will he find any true Vasylli left?

From "A New History of the Covenant" by Dar-in-Exile
Mirnían II

CHAPTER 1
LLUN THE SMITH

L lun the Smith gazed into the fire. The bellows blew, and the sparks exploded before him like a shower of fireflies. He breathed in. The smell—soot, sweat, dross melting from pure metal. It was as near paradise as anyone could get in Vasyllia. Especially after Vasyllia fell.

"Smith Llun! How much longer?"

It was the fifth time Garmun had asked the same question in the last half hour. The old fool. Llun was continually amazed that the fat man was the most sought-after master builder in Vasyllia. All he ever seemed to do was sit in Llun's smithy, covering most of it with his belly.

"It's coming, it's coming," growled Llun. He didn't mind Garmun sitting around while he worked. But no one...no one was allowed to break the hallowed moments when the fire and the metal fused to become something new, something sacred.

"By the Great Father, Llun, I only asked for nails, not works of art."

Llun twitched at the name. *Great Father, my muscular left bicep. Why is the Raven renaming himself now, of all times? Does he imagine we've forgotten how he took everything from us?*

"What is it about you master builders? What ails you? Too many children?"

Garmun turned purple, opened his mouth to speak, then choked on himself. He had no wife, but his illegitimate progeny filled half of Vasyllia's first reach. Crude people snickered that being so fat was normal after so many pregnancies.

"Peace, Brother Garmun," said Llun. "They're all but done. And I promise you they'll be the hardiest, longest-lasting nails you'll find in all Vasyllia."

And the only ones with a raven etched on the nail's head. May his memory be forever cursed, and may every hammer stroke hasten the time of his demise...

"You mean the most *exquisite* nails in Vasyllia, no doubt," the fat man complained. "I've never seen anyone so taken with his own talent. Don't you know that your little frills and personal touches make no difference? Competence! Competence! That's what the market wants."

"The market, with all its frippery and cheap wares, can burn in the fires of the land of the dead for all I care." It slipped out. Llun hoped the hammer would be distraction enough. But he had never been blessed by fortune.

"Your talk smacks of the Outer Lands, you fool. Be careful no one in the Great Father's good graces overhears you."

"Overhears what?" said a new voice from the doorway.

The stranger who walked in was the antithesis of Garmun—short and wiry like a ratter. Everything about him suggested potential action—his smile, just on the verge of malice, his hands, holding his thick belt as though it were someone's throat, the sharp line of his cheekbones, suggesting some nomad blood. His physicality was so overwhelming that it almost distracted from the dog's scalp hanging from his belt.

So this must be one of that new department that the Gumiren—those filthy nomad invaders from the South—had concocted for collaborators. What was it called? The Consistory, yes. The secret police of the Raven. Dog-men, the commons called them. A kind name for a traitor against his own people.

"I'm not open to new customers," said Llun, trying to keep his tone light.

"That's a relief," the stranger said, with more gentleness than Llun expected. "No one will bother us, then."

He closed the door and dropped the black curtain over the door-window.

"What a pleasant smithy you have here, Brother Llun."

Llun stiffened as the stranger began to look around the smithy. Like a bitch on the scent, the stranger's pointed face bore down on the cluttered left counter of the smithy. He pulled out two interlacing shields of iron leaf-work tracery so fine they almost looked woven. Each held a heraldic icon of a raven in flight.

"Well, that's..." He didn't finish, but to Llun's surprise it sounded like he was about to say "beautiful." What? A Raven's man actually admiring beauty for its own sake?

Llun's stomach churned. It was all wrong: there was genuine admiration in the stranger's eyes. He appreciated the shields as things of beauty, not as objects to buy or sell. That wasn't supposed to happen. The Raven's men followed a script. They were supposed to ask where Llun was going to sell these useless trinkets, and when he hemmed and hawed about beauty and artistry, they would threaten Llun with something horrible.

Llun had seen enough of the Gumiren's work to know that the threats of the collaborators were never idle—weavers with one eye burned out just so their depth perception would no longer be of any use, sword-wrights with their right hands chopped off at the wrist, potters with broken feet.

Damn them all, he thought bitterly.

But this one was admiring decorative shields that had no practical use whatsoever. Llun had made them merely for the sake of beauty.

"What possessed you to make such a thing?"

Llun's hammer stopped in mid-air. It was the choice of words. "Possessed." No, this was no mere inquisitor. This man understood the creative process. What it means to make something, and how it feels to be taken by the hand of the Maker.

"It made itself," said Llun, hesitating. "I was just the instrument."

The stranger gasped with pleasure, as though Llun's words had given him a taste of something he hadn't felt in a very long time. Maybe this was an impostor? A motley fool who put on the dog-scalp to ridicule the Consistory? But such people did not walk the streets for long before their bodies were used as decorations for lamp-posts.

"Llun," said the dog-man, and looked Llun directly in the eyes.

The lack of the "Brother" before Llun's name frightened him more than the direct gaze. This collaborator was something new. Yes, he was likely an artist. An artist of torture and death.

"Llun, you stand there, gawking like a fool, telling me you made something for the sheer pleasure of artistry?"

The stranger's right index finger caressed the outline of the raven, as though he could memorize shapes better with his finger. Could he see it, the *true* picture? The hammer slipped in Llun's hand and almost landed on his thumb. *Careful...*

"Yes." Llun's voice didn't remain as steady as he would have liked. The stranger noticed. His smile was an adder's smile.

"Who taught you to waste your time like this?"

So they had come to it at last. The stranger wanted Llun to be an informer to the collaborators, a friend of the dogs.

Not on my life.

"No one," said Llun, continuing to beat the nails. "Don't think I use my work-time on these things. I give all the Great Father's time to my customers, as anyone, even fat Garmun here, will tell you." The builder looked like he wanted to kill Llun and run away from him at the same time. "I do this...art...in my own time."

The stranger raised his eyebrows slightly, faintly amused. Llun immediately realized his mistake. He shouldn't have said anything about having the luxury of time for himself.

"What a shame," said the Consistory man. "You should *rest* during your free time, Brother Llun. It will help you make better nails and horseshoes and braziers. *Useful* things. Will you accept a gift from the Great Father? A gratis pass to one of the houses of rest?"

The dog-man leered. Llun flushed, embarrassed. Did the dog-man really think that sort of thing appealed to an artisan? How typical. The smith working off his frustrations with a romp in the hay.

Llun struck the nail so hard it cracked in half.

"I don't fraternize with prostitutes," said Llun. His finger bled where the cracked nail had pierced it. *Concentrate!*

The Consistory man smiled, gentle as ever. "I didn't say a thing about *fraternizing*. And why use such a crude word as prostitute? I believe I have heard them better described as purveyors of pleasure."

Garmun chortled, then tried to disappear. For a man of his size, that was not easy.

"Anyway, I don't have time for that nonsense," said Llun.

"Nonsense? It is all sanctioned by our Great Father himself. Are you suggesting that anything his greatness allows is not worthy of your time? I will not say coin, because I have already offered you a gratis pass."

"That is not what I meant to say." Llun stopped hammering, put the hammer down, and wiped his hands on his apron, which only made them dirtier. "I'm sorry, I don't believe I have the honor of your name, Brother?"

That should bring matters to a head, whether or not Llun's head would be the cost.

"Ah, my mistake! My name is Aspidían. You may have heard of me."

Oh, *Heights*. Aspidían? The right hand of Yadovír, the traitor who had opened the gates of Vasyllia to the invading army of Gumiren. Some even insinuated that Aspidían was more than his right hand. By all accounts, he was a monster that had killed over one hundred true Vasylli with his own hands.

"Brother Llun." Aspidían's face no longer showed interest in anything. He leaned against the wall in assumed fatigue, the very picture of a man who had seen too much and wished merely to be left alone. "I would be most honored if you would come to the Consistory's halls on the morrow, perhaps at three hours after sunrise? I would like to employ your skills in a most impor-tant matter. Good day to you."

"As you say, Brother Aspidían."

As soon as he left, the forge coughed, the bellows sighed, the anvil begged to be struck again. Everything in the smithy heaved out a relieved breath. Garmun was near to tears of hysteria.

"Brother Llun, Brother Llun," he whispered, as if expecting the inquisitor to be eavesdropping just outside the door. "Do you know what this means?" He threw his hands up above his head. "Who will make things for me now? Don't you know you are the best craftsman in Vasyllia? Have I ever told you that, Brother? Have I?" Both sweaty hands, fleshy and fat, wrung Llun's arm, kneading it like bread, though even his massive hands hardly encircled the width of Llun's arm, hardened by years of the smithy. "Why must it be you? I know the Great Father needs an occasional example for everyone's instruction, but ... why *you*?"

"Calm yourself, you fat fool. Why not take the man at his word? Perhaps there is some manner of work to be done?"

Garmun guffawed. "You madman of an artist! Don't you know what they do to people like you? Have you forgotten Dashun?"

Llun tried to stop the grimace, but failed. Why did Garmun have to mention Dashun of all people? Llun was sure he would never forget the sight of Dashun's mutilated body. But what was worse? The torture, or the way he had publicly recanted all his beliefs and convictions? He had read aloud a text prepared for him by the Raven. Then he had collaborated with them, even uncovered a conspiracy against the Gumiren. And still they killed him horribly.

"You exaggerate," Llun said, coughing to cover the quaver in his voice. "I'm no danger to anyone. I am simply an odd, self-absorbed craftsman."

"Brother Llun, do you know *anything* about Aspidían?" He raised both hands, palms out. The gesture to ward off evil.

"Your nails, Brother Garmun."

"Brother Llun. Oh, my dear friend." Garmun wept, blubbering like a woman. Perversely, Llun remembered the jesting commoners and the purported pregnancies. He couldn't help himself.

"There, there, Garmun. I know it's common enough to cry more than usual when you're pregnant."

Garmun turned purple again. Shoving Llun back so that he nearly flew into the forge itself, he pointed a finger thick as a blood sausage at his nose. "You ... you ..." He huffed out like a passing thunderstorm, taking his bombast with him.

Llun remembered to breathe.

"You can come out now," he whispered. The entire left side of the table heaved. "Did no one teach you discretion, you little idiot?"

"Llun," said the girl of thirteen who finally managed to extricate herself from all the bits of metal. "Did you mean what you said to Garmun? Or did you just make him mad so he wouldn't be associated with you when you're trussed up like a chicken on the spit?"

"Which do you think, Mirodara?"

Mirodara's face went white. "I wasn't serious, Llun."

"Never mind. I'm not that worried. I'm not nearly as important as your father was."

"Dashun is *not* my father. I have no father. Not after he collaborated."

"You can't wash his blood from inside you, girl! Why do you

think they've been after you all this time?"

Llun's breath caught as he realized how close the girl had been to death only a few moments ago. Was *that* why Aspidían had come in? Was someone blabbing again?

"Anyway, I don't even look like Dashun. Everyone knows I'm my mother's—"

"Don't!" Llun's voice cracked. The last thing he wanted was to be reminded of Vatrina.

"I'm sorry," said Mirodara, her face switching from red to white and back to red with dizzying speed. "I know you don't like to talk about her. But she was my *mother*, Llun. You're just her brother."

"You don't have any siblings, Mirodara. You don't know. You just don't know. I never knew either of my parents."

"Yes, yes, and now I'm the only one you have left. Blah blah blah. You won't talk me out of it."

"What do you hope to accomplish, anyway, with these...what do they call themselves?"

"The Sons of the Swan. We're going to reclaim Vasyllia for Darina Sabíana, the true queen of all the lands. She's still alive in that palace. I *know* it."

Llun laughed.

"You laugh? You're about to be thrown into the middle of it all. You think they'll let you stay on the side, uninvolved?"

Llun sighed and stretched his aching shoulders. Mirodara, for all her silliness, was older than her years. She had no choice. All the children had grown older the day Vasyllia fell.

"You'll stay here tonight," said Llun, the tone of finality clear in his voice. Mirodara looked like she wanted to argue, but nodded and extended a hand to Llun.

"Peace?"

Llun embraced her, trying hard not to weep. She did look just like her mother, his sister.

Please, Adonais. If you still listen to us who failed you, don't let them take her. Not her. She's just a girl.

On the day of blood, a day when the sun turns black and stars fall as flames from the sky, those walking the streets of the Great City will seem alive. But they are naught but the hordes of the dead. In that day, the swan's wing will be broken, and the falcon will be too far to hear her cries of pain. The earth itself will moan for the Healer. But the Healer is lost in the maze of his own doubts...

From "The Prophecy of Llun"
(The Sayings, Book XXIII 3:1-3)

CHAPTER 2
THE CONSISTORY

The early morning light showed Llun's smithy off at its best. The prevailing colors peeking through the soot-grimed windows were gold and orange. No customer came this early, and as the sun rose, the true, hidden beauty of the place came to life. In the light of the fire, the smithy danced with shadows, but the morning sun, which coddled like a mother and warmed like childhood memory, showed the things Llun made in their true aspect.

He picked up the decorative shields that Aspidían had so admired. Only now could their secret be told, their mystery uncovered. They were not ravens at all in the tracery. The morning rays, coming through the window at a very specific angle, revealed the ravens to be two falcons. The dancing fire-light of any house's interior was intended to trick the casual observer to think they were ravens depicted flying at the observer, head feathers curiously ruffled by the wind. The figure was made so that it shifted in the mind's eye after long contemplation in the light of morning, like a difficult sentence in a book that rewards the slow reader. Then, the ravens transformed into falcons.

Llun wondered if Aspidían had read the riddle in the tracery.

Was that why he was so astounded? Or was it true appreciation? It was bad enough not to have any visible representation of the Raven in his smithy, as was required by the so-called Great Father. But to blaspheme him by association with something as unclean as the falcon—the sigil of Voran, the Healer and the great enemy of the Raven—that would be reason enough for a high inquisitor to pay a visit to the first reach of Vasyllia. Or was it simply that someone had reported Llun in hopes of gaining his smithy as a reward? Llun knew of too many such cases to consider it impossible.

Too many thoughts. Like someone banging an iron pan with a wooden spoon inside his head. Llun decided to take the long way to the Consistory.

He looked in on Mirodara sleeping in the back room. She was sprawled on the floor, snoring. As though she had not a care in the world. He couldn't help smiling, though that only brought back the pain of memory. The way her nose bent slightly to the left, giving her mouth a soft quirk, as though she were always on the verge of laughter—that was her mother's most obvious feature. Rubbing his eyes until the stars exploded on the inside of his eyelids, he hurried out into the street.

I will not be maudlin this early in the morning, he thought.

He still thought of his smithy as belonging to the first reach. Only a few houses down, Siloán the potter's home stood, now even smaller-looking than usual after the mead-house had swallowed two neighboring houses to become the largest building in the reach. The roads were as meandering, the refuse as omnipresent. The poor still bickered at street corners, fighting for the rights to an intersection as though their eternal soul depended on it. But it wasn't the first reach any more, he reminded himself. Just a few roads down was the new merchants' quarter—part of the "Great Father's" efforts at equalizing opportunities for all citizens. Or some such unintelligible nonsense.

The walls that had stood between the three reaches of Vasyllia for centuries had been torn down. The stairways joining them together now seemed naked without the walls buttressing them. They were a pitiful sight, and most Vasylli instinctively avoided the stairs, preferring the new, wide gravel roads that joined all reaches in stark, over-straight lines, so counterintuitive to the gentle roll and sway of the mountain's side.

In the other direction from the merchants' quarter was the other great equalizer—the pleasure quarter, as it was officially labeled. Llun flushed with sudden disgust, remembering the dogman's offer. The air of the first reach had always been redolent with aroma. But it had been good and clean, for all its earthiness. The first reach had had its problems, but people had been principled, keeping to a code that separated them from the corruption of the upper reaches. It had been important before, to keep oneself clean of the base and the vile. Now, worker and noble alike drank sour ale in the wide anterooms of the whore-houses. Equality indeed.

The former second reach was now a shambling mess. Most of Nebesta's refugees still lived there in tottering canvas tents. Every hundred paces or so, a pile of those tents was set apart from the next by a line of spears stuck into the earth, their points directed at the people in the camps. Guards with longbows patrolled the spear-lines constantly. Whenever they passed, silence fell.

Cutting into the silence like a knife into flesh was the sound of children. Two Nebesti boys, dressed in barely anything but loincloths, chased a much smaller boy through the pile of tents, screaming something menacing. The small boy turned directly toward the lines of spears. Llun felt his vision go dim as he saw that none of them were stopping. Two grim Vasylli warriors converged toward them. One of them grabbed a standing spear from the ground and pointed it at the children, shaking it menacingly.

The children tried to stop, but their momentum was considerable. The first one—a ratty-haired boy of about six or seven— managed to dig his heels at a suitable distance. But his assailants, who were both muscular and seemed large for their age, were not as quick to stop. They scratched and pulled at each other, trying to stop in time. At the very last moment, even the Vasylli guard paled. But he didn't move.

The small boy, pushed toward the spear, managed to twist aside at the last minute. He wasn't impaled.

But his side was slashed open. There was a lot of blood, even from the distance where Llun stood, clutching his chest for horror. A young Nebesti man ran into Llun's field of vision, his hands shaking in those ridiculously expansive gestures that all Nebesti indulge in. Behind him was a young woman. She stopped as soon as she saw the boy. Her sunburned face blanched, and she screamed.

The warriors tensed as the Nebesti man approached them. The warrior who had not hurt the boy stood in front of the one who had. His fists were bunched, and he yelled at the Nebesti to back down. The father did not. His eyes' whites grew, and his hands waved more and more frantically. All the while, he moved toward the spears. The second warrior drew his sword, yelling. Llun couldn't make out the words in the general mayhem of women and children screaming. The stricken boy moaned not at all, which was even more frightening. The father shoved his face into the warrior's face, his raspy torrent of words turning into shouting. The warrior's eyes bulged, and his face grew red. He kept repeating something again and again. Not once did he look at the boy.

Something twanged by Llun's ear. The boy's father twisted back unnaturally and fell to the ground. An arrow shivered in his shoulder.

"Move along!" A rough voice yelled near Llun. A huge Gumir, his face twisted into a grimace, making his already angled eyes disappear in the folds of his dirt-brown face. "Not your concern, Vasylli. Great Father's business. Move along."

Llun looked away and moved along. As he walked, he heard the familiar laugh of the Gumiren as they closed in. Then the thudding began. The sounds of fists on flesh and bone. Gritting his teeth, Llun ran on.

Where the Covenant Tree had once stood, a pile of kindling reached as high as a two-story house. It stood as a dour reminder of that day Vasyllia fell, when the Gumiren had nearly thrown the children of Adonais's faithful into the fire. It had been a cruel joke of the Raven. Deny your divinity, your Adonais, he had said. And I will spare your children. And for what? For an existence of fear and no hope of a brighter future? Perhaps it would have been better for the children to burn.

Above the pile of logs—it obscenely resembled a huge raven's nest—was the Raven's totem: a stone obelisk that branched out into a pair of jagged wings. It was black as obsidian, but without that stone's glass-like sheen. Whatever it was made of, the material seemed to suck light in, making it not so much black as absent—a hole in the fabric of the world shaped like an obelisk.

Llun stood before it, his hatred a hair's edge from boiling. He forced himself to move on toward the third reach.

Of all the former reaches, the third was the one least affected by the Gumiren. Most of the damage of the battle for Vasyllia had been quickly repaired, as the Gumiren took residence in the mansions of the wealthy third-reachers. Many of them had kept the nobles as their servants. More like slaves, in fact, especially the women. Some old noblemen had been quietly dispatched during the now-infamous "night purges" that the Gumiren conducted every so often. Llun had heard that the purges continued, but now it was not the Gumiren, but turncoat Vasylli who would rat out their own brothers for a chance at a better set of table knives.

Seeing the mansions still sparkling like the jewels of great Vasyllia that was—it gave Llun vertigo. For a brief, brilliant moment it seemed that everything—the Gumiren overlords, the horrors of the nightly purges, the baseness to which everything had sunk—was just a dream. After all, wasn't the palace of the

Dar still standing, its seven towers like beacons of hope leading toward a glorious future?

Except now the palace was the dwelling place of a demonic Power who had the brazenness to call himself everyone's father.

～

The gates to the outer courtyard of the palace, which now housed the Consistory, used to be open at all times as a sign of the Dar's closeness to his people. After the fall of Vasyllia, the gates had been shut. So, when they opened to admit Llun, he had the sinking feeling that he was being invited to step into the gullet of a hungry monster.

He had been inside once only, during the matriculation ceremony of the warrior seminary. In the old days. He, as one of the preferred swordsmiths of the seminary, had received a place of honor in a front row of the viewing gallery. It was an impressive sight—the pentagonal courtyard filled with silent, unmoving, black-robed warriors, all with their swords drawn. At the whip-like calls of their cohort elders, the hundreds of warriors had demonstrated, as one man, every step of the sword-forms. It was like a dance, and it had taken his breath away.

Now, he was struck by the emptiness of the square, save for a few scurrying forms of servants. Instead, his eyes were drawn to the huge banners flapping on the walls of the keep—the red raven obelisk on a black field. Like a bad joke, Sabíana's sign of the gold sun on black field flitted small and insignificant from a pole jutting up above the smallest of the seven towers.

Perhaps she is alive, he thought. The thought did little to comfort him. What was a crippled young woman with no army behind her supposed to do to change the fortunes of Vasyllia?

"What, you as well?" Aspidían materialized out of nowhere. "It's the strangest thing, Brother Llun. Whenever one of you old Vasylli come up here (oh, it's rare enough, I grant you) their eye is always drawn to that pitiful banner. I wonder why?"

"Brother Aspidían," said Llun, bowing in greeting. The wiry inquisitor was dressed in simple linen trousers with a billowing linen overshirt—the picture of leisure and relaxation. Only his eyes still smoldered behind his smile.

"Come, Brother Llun. I want you to meet someone."

They took an unobtrusive door in the keep's wall that led to a twisting staircase. It was dusty and disused, and Llun was sure that this was where he would be suddenly attacked from behind and thrown into a dungeon. Instead, at the top of the staircase, Aspidían opened another unobtrusive door. Facing the golden light that streamed into the stairwell was like staring into the sun. When Llun's eyes adjusted, he saw they were in a vaulted chamber covered in frescoes. Every inch of the curved ceilings and walls burst with giant-sized fancies on the theme of flowers and birds. Bumblebees painted with actual gold leaf seemed to buzz on purple and red petals of peonies. Strawberries and blueberries burst from the confines of their green and yellow leaves.

"He likes it. How pleasant."

Llun's stomach lurched at the sound of that voice. It was more than one voice. It was like a voice with a hundred echoes, coming from one mouth. When he saw the speaker, it took a strong effort of will not to cringe.

He was...well, beautiful. Flawless skin, like polished ivory. Soft eyes, almost lavender colored. Long-fingered hands, the nails reflecting the golden candlelight in the room like polished metal. Llun had heard that Yadovír, the Mouth of the Raven, had grown younger and more pleasing to look at in the five years since the fall of Vasyllia. But the beauty was somehow... wrong. As he stared at Yadovír, unable to look away, it seemed to Llun that something shivered in his face. No, *under* his face. Like his entire surface—skin, face, hands—was an elaborate costume for something foul underneath.

Yadovír cocked his head to one side and slitted his eyes, assessing. "You're a bear of a man, aren't you? But my friend here says that you have talent."

"That he does," said Aspidían, coming close to Yadovír. *Too close.* Llun felt sick to his stomach.

Yadovír's eyes wandered over Llun, from head to foot, lingering. He smiled, a predator's smile that was not his own. Llun had the sensation that he was being judged as potential food.

"For all your strength, Brother Llun," said Yadovír, with a hint of a growl. "You are rather soft, aren't you?"

Aspidían chuckled, and they both turned away from Llun and walked to a strange contrivance in the middle of the room. It was so out of character with the general opulence that at first Llun didn't understand what he was looking at. The he realized it was a hole. In the floorboards. In that hole was a hearth, the simple kind that you find in a first-reacher house. There were pillows around the hearth—simple, red pillows of no especial value. A small table stood by the hearth. Three goblets and mead. Mead? Llun couldn't understand what he was seeing. Why, in this palatial room, was there a sliver of commonness more appropriate to Llun's own back room behind the forge?

Aspidían and Yadovír sat on two of the cushions, leaning into one another in a way that bespoke more than casual intimacy. It was unsettling. The whole picture was unsettling. Was this part of an elaborate plan to confuse him so much that he would somehow stumble into revealing some dangerous truth? Did they know about Mirodara?

"Why do you gawk?" Aspidían guffawed. "Sit. That cushion's for you."

Llun did as he was told. Yadovír continued to look at him hungrily as Aspidían poured him the mead. Llun tried to focus his attention on the cup, and once again he lost himself in the quality of the work. The wrought iron tracery woven like ivy around the wooden goblet was exquisite. It nearly rivaled his own abilities. Then he drank the mead and nearly drowned in the pleasure of that taste. He had not had good mead—hearty, first-reacher bread-ale—in years.

Laughter jolted him out of his contemplation.

"You're right, Aspidían," said Yadovír. "He really is...an artist."

Llun felt his face get warm, and suddenly he was angry. Sick of it all. His teeth creaked as he tensed his jaw.

"What do you want of me?" he asked, surprised at the audible growl in his own voice.

"Oh, how disappointing," drawled Yadovír. "No small talk? Cut straight to the heart of the matter, eh? Artists." He sounded faintly disgusted with the idea.

"You never understood us," said Aspidían. "We operate on a different schedule than most. Don't we, Brother Llun?"

Llun refused to be included in the offer of intimacy. He had no desire to be named the kind of artist that Aspidían was. If they wanted something of him, they would have to pry it out of his hands. The thought gave him shivers.

"As you wish," said Yadovír, putting his cup down, then yawning as he stretched against Aspidían, who still seemed amused by everything. "We want you to take on a commission. For the Consistory. In fact, we want it to be the last commission you take."

There was a double meaning there, Llun knew it. But he pretended not to hear it. "You want me to be your exclusive smith? But why?"

"We have a...sudden vacancy." Aspidían's eyebrows came together, shadowing his eyes.

Llun picked up his cup and offered it to them, significantly.

"Yes," said Yadovír. "These cups are his work. As you see, he was very good. But he had an unfortunate slip in judgment. He can no longer help us."

"You killed him?"

Yadovír looked disappointed. "No, of course not. They only took his hand. The Gumiren."

"So...wait, I'm not sure I understand. Are you saying that you and the Gumiren are not...on the same side?"

Aspidían's eyes were no longer smoldering. They burned.

"Now *that* is a comment unworthy of you, Brother Llun. What makes you think any Vasylli would willingly collaborate with those animals? No. Compromises were made, yes. Necessary ones. But never think, not for a moment, that we do not anticipate with great joy the moment when we can slaughter them in their beds."

"What about the Raven?" said Llun.

Aspidían tensed, and his hand went to his boot. Something gleamed there.

"Do...not...utter—" he whispered menacingly.

"Oh, don't worry, Aspidían," said Yadovír. "He's brave, for all of his goggling at the fine things in life. Perhaps not as soft as we thought." His smile stretched his face. "Brother Llun, I'll let you say it once. But never again. The *Great Father*, for your information, is well on his way to becoming a figure of speech. Soon the Vasylli will forget about the Raven. Just as he would want it. His desire is not Vasyllia itself. It is something else. He has promised me that, soon, we will have Vasyllia back to ourselves."

"How can you trust him? He seems willing enough to turn on those he needed to get into Vasyllia in the first place."

"I don't trust him, you fool," said Yadovír. Something shimmered in the shadows behind him—a suggestion of huge, jagged wings. Llun's heart plunged to his ankles. "I'm useful to him. And I'm making the Gumiren less so. Soon, their time will be over."

"And high time too," said Aspidían. "They've all become so fat and complacent. The Ghan himself can hardly walk now, he is so round. He must be carried around on a litter."

Llun's curiosity got the better of him. "Is it true, what's been said in the first reach? That there are troubles in the Gumiren ruling council?"

Aspidían put on an entirely new face. Intense concentration, with a hint of anticipation. Llun had a suspicion that was the sincerest Aspidían face yet. "Do tell, Brother Llun. What sort of gossip are the commons bandying about?"

Llun resented the tone, but forced himself to speak evenly.

"Well, in the first years of the occupation, the Gumiren were everywhere, weren't they? Patrolling streets, eating at the public houses, propping up the spear lines in the refugee camp. But over the years, fewer and fewer of them were seen in the lower reaches. Then the rumors started that the Gumiren had taken to Vasylli luxuries. Particularly wine and mead. Not surprising, given their nomad bloodlines. And they were willing to give more and more of the ruling responsibilities to the collaborators."

Yadovír smiled again, and Llun realized he had said "collaborators" out loud. *Focus, you idiot!*

"Then there are the rumors of diseases among the Gumiren. Some sort of pox, some say. Others are less...compassionate in their guesses."

"Yes, you could say that," said Aspidían, snickering. "Why are you so afraid to say it out loud, Llun? Your tongue won't be polluted. Say it. 'Venereal diseases.'" He mouthed it, slowly, as if he could taste the syllables.

Llun scowled.

"To answer your question, Brother Llun," said Yadovír, "yes, the Gumiren are growing complacent. And soon, soon the time will come when we will take back Vasyllia for the Vasylli. I ask you now. Will you help us? Will you help your people?"

This was not collaboration with the enemy at all. This was... well, this was exactly what Llun wanted. But not with Yadovír. He was there during the battle for Vasyllia. He remembered what Yadovír had done. Yadovír had orchestrated a pogrom of clerics of the cult of Adonais to cover up his own crimes, his own treachery. The thought propped up his cold hatred, and the words tumbled out of his mouth even as he thought them.

"And what about the Darina? Where is she in all your plans?"

The silence hissed, so complete that Llun heard the squelching sound of Yadovír's feral smile stretching across his gums.

"She is...instrumental."

"She is alive, then?"

"Oh, yes. Very much so."

"I don't believe you."

Aspidían got up, slowly, his muscles so taut that it looked like an invisible hand lifted him up, like a marionette. "You don't seem to understand, Brother Llun. Here we are, extending you a hand of friendship when you know very well that we could be extending a corkscrew to separate your nails from your hands. And you spit on this hand of friendship? Is that wise? Do you not understand who it is that sits before you?"

Llun's breath quickened. His head buzzed. He had had too much of the mead. Or was there something in the mead? Something to make him more...malleable?

"I...forgive me, Brother Aspidían," said Llun, nearly whimpering, and hating himself for it. "I...why me? Why choose me to be your exclusive smith? You have seen my work. It is good, yes. But I do not work fast. And if you need a swordsmith for an uprising against the Gumiren...well, you would not have many swords..."

Aspidían relaxed back into Yadovír's side. "He has a point, you know," he said, conversationally.

"You forget one thing." Yadovír looked at Aspidían. "Who he *is*."

"Ah yes!" Aspidían's eyes sparkled with mischief as he crossed his arms across his chest. "You are related to key members of the Sons of the Swan."

And there it was. The trap snapped shut. Llun almost imagined the sound, like a big bear trap chomping down on his ankle. He nearly panicked then and there.

"Dashun is dead," Llun managed to say, barely containing his fear within. "His infection has been cut out of Vasyllia. I am not of their mind. I do not seek what they seek."

"No, but Mirodara does," said Yadovír.

"She is a *child!*"

"Children will grow to be men and women, a new generation

of rot at the heart of Vasyllia. Until every Son of the Swan is killed, no peace will ever last here or anywhere else in the world."

"Unless..." Aspidían cut in, his voice reasonable and kind. "We are prepared to overlook her involvement with the Sons as ... a youthful indiscretion. But only if you take up our offer."

Llun sighed. "Am I expected to give an answer immediately?"

"No, no!" Aspidían waved his hands placatingly. "Take your time. Just ... not too much of it."

The dawn of hope rises. From the dirt of the tree's roots will arise a sleeper of ages. She will be braver than many men, stronger than myriad warriors. Her age is not counted in years, but in the bitter days of pain and loss. Her death will bring forth life. Her sleep will make Living Water flow again in the wasteland...

From "The Prophecy of Llun"
(The Sayings, Book XXIII, 5:8-10)

CHAPTER 3
MIRODARA

L lun hardly remembered the way he took back to his smithy. It didn't help that most of Vasyllia was hidden in fog, dropping the early summer temperatures down to what they had been in late spring. The kind of weather that obscured one's thoughts and deadened one's limbs.

Bacon. The smell shocked him back to awareness. He was nearly home, and the bacon-smell, to his amazement, was not coming from the mead-house, but from his own smithy. He laughed with pleasure. It had been a long time since he had eaten bacon.

Mirodara.

Idiot girl. Is this your idea of being unobtrusive?

He rushed into the smithy, and the smoke attacked his eyes and mouth. He choked as the pleasing smell of fried pig transformed into the sickly-sweet smell of burnt pig.

"If you're going to let the whole neighborhood know you're here, at least don't burn the bacon!" He smiled as he saw Mirodara blowing on a thin, black piece of something that could have once been edible. She breathed out in exasperation and offered him a bite. He shook his head and laughed.

"I wanted to make you something nice," she said, never more like his sister than at that moment.

"If you really want to do something nice for me, you'll sit down and listen."

She straightened at the change in Llun's voice. Nodding slowly, she threw the charred bit of meat back into the pan on the hearth. It sizzled, as though hurtling a final insult at her.

"So ..." she began, "what sort of false promises did they make, the vipers?"

"Stop." He raised his voice just enough for her to curl in on herself a little. "I said listen. Open mind, yes?"

"Fine." He saw that she was working very hard not to sulk.

"They know about you. Not about the Sons in general. About you, Mirodara."

"Then why am I still here?"

Llun sighed and looked away from her. He suddenly, ridiculously, really wanted to eat that bacon.

"Oh, I see," she said, her voice husky. "They're using me to force you to do something. What, exactly?"

"I'm not entirely sure, to be honest. They say they need a swordsmith. But I can't imagine why they'd want me for that. Unless Yadovír wants a family heirloom he can hang over his door."

"Yes, you do take rather a bit more time than necessary on ... well, everything. Even nails!" She chuckled.

"I think there's much that they're not telling me. But one thing I know for sure. If you do not stop your silly association with the Sons of the Swan, it'll be the end of both of us."

Mirodara took Llun's paw of a hand between her own. They were so uncalloused and small. Like a mouse holding on to a lion. Llun's heart felt stretched to a breaking point.

"Llun, let's be honest. They're going to get us, sooner or later. Whether or not you help them. Whether or not I ever so much as speak to a Son of the Swan again. At some point, in the middle of the night, you'll be taken in your sleep. Me too."

"Don't speak like that. I'll—"

"What matters," she said, not listening to him, "is what we manage to do before they stop us. What have either of us done in our lives that is worth remembering? Hm? But now, when our world has already ended, now ... well, every decision of every person can have huge consequences. Don't you understand that? Every person who capitulates to the Gumiren and their collaborators is guilty of treachery before our whole people. But every single child who refuses to bow down...How can I make you understand? Every sacrifice...it matters. Even if it seems pointless. It *matters*."

"When did you grow up, my little cub?" He tried to smile through the tears that now fell. He wiped them off. "But what if I were to tell you..." He lowered his voice to a whisper. "There are rumblings ... that the collaborators are preparing to throw off the Gumiren. To restore Vasyllia to the Vasylli. Even to restore the Darina to her place."

"You believe them? They'll say anything, Llun. Have you forgotten what they did?"

"I haven't, no. *You* were too small to remember, I would have thought."

"I was nothing of the sort. I saw the warriors ... *our* warriors turn into beasts. I saw them attack defenseless women who tried to reason with them, to prevent them from hacking down every priest in sight. You don't forget such a sight. Not ever. And these are the people you entrust the safety of our city to?"

"You're right. I just can't fathom losing you."

"You'll have to fathom a lot more than that. Don't you understand? This isn't the battle for Vasyllia. It's the battle for the soul of Vasyllia."

She breathed deeply, as though considering whether or not to divulge something.

"There's something else," she said. "It's Voran, the son of Otchigen."

"What about him?" Llun couldn't help the bitterness coming

through. Voran, Darina Sabíana's intended and the supposed hope of Vasyllia's reclamation, had been exiled years ago. But rumors had trickled into Vasyllia that he had found Living Water and that he was using it to heal those who had fallen to the Gumiren onslaught. Others suggested that he was gathering an army to reclaim Vasyllia. Probably all of it was rubbish.

"The Sons have it on excellent authority that he is finally coming back to Vasyllia. And he has Living Water."

Llun couldn't muster the enthusiasm necessary to believe her. He found he had run out of things to say. She hugged him.

"I want to go out in a blaze of glory. I want to do something so mad that the Heights will have no choice but to bow down again before my act of courage. You'll see. It'll happen soon. Everything is going to change very soon."

How horribly have you grown up, my little one, Llun thought. *Can I expect anything else, when all you've ever known is fear and death?*

The Day of Blood will be dread and awful. But it is not the end of the tribulation. Hear my voice, O faithful of Vasyllia! There will come a time when brother will slaughter father, for he will not recognize his face. Brown-faced Gumir will attack white-faced Vasylli, but he will be stabbed in his back. No one will know the face of his enemy in the darkness and the chaos. Nor will he know the face of his friend.

From "The Prophecy of Llun"
(The Sayings, Book XXIII, 2:4-7)

CHAPTER 4
THE SONS OF THE SWAN

After Mirodara left, Llun could not face his thoughts. He opened the smithy and threw himself into his work with the kind of abandon he had only really felt in the early days, when his body hardly noticed the strain of smithing. It was a surprise to him when he looked at the window to see that it had gone completely dark.

He allowed his forge to sputter and die. The shadows at first faintly resisted their inevitable end, then they lay down to a quiet death. He went to his rest in the back room, bare as always but for the bench lining the back wall. The barrenness was a comfort, clearing the mind, especially in its contrast to the clutter in the smithy itself. Llun lay down on the bench, not bothering to undress. In spite of the buzzing of his mind, he could not keep his eyelids open, and only a few moments later, he was asleep.

When his door tore from its hinges, he woke with a start. There were five men in his room, dressed in black, a shriveled dog's head hanging from the belt of each. In the absurd confusion of the just-awoken, all Llun could think of was how disappointing it was that the promise of bacon had not lived up to the reality. The intruders gave him no time to reflect. They all fell on top of him like the dogs that they were.

He struggled, but it was soon obvious that any sign of resistance meant an excuse for them to inflict unnecessary pain. But pain was an old friend of Llun's. He fought them back as furiously as a cornered rat. They were in *his* smithy. He knew better than they where the most painful weapons were, if only he could get to them.

Two held Llun's arms pinned to his back, while two more demonstratively took off their gloves. Underneath, Llun saw black metal between their fingers. This was not a mere arrest, then. He was to be made an example of.

Not in my smithy.

He made a feint of losing consciousness, forcing the two holding him to lean down to keep him pinned. As he leaned hard against the shin of the man holding his right hand, he twisted into him, catching his foot under him and pushing his knee back. Llun felt it crack, and the man howled. Before the others could restrain him, Llun lifted both his attackers up with his huge body and threw them at the rest of their fellows.

Under his sleeping bench, Llun kept a half-done war hammer. It was too heavy for most men to lift, but in the heat of the struggle he lifted it like a dry twig and swung with all his force at his assailants. Something gave way behind the blow. More wailing. For the briefest of moments, Llun saw a way through the five attackers as they tried to avoid his blows. Dealers of pain were always the worst at bearing it themselves, he knew. Llun rushed past them, through the broken doorway, into the smithy proper. It was still dark, except for the gaping hole where the butchers had broken in. Llun ran through it, but stopped dead in his tracks.

Unaccountably, it had snowed last night. The moon being full, the thin layer of pristine white seemed to give off its own eerie light. In the dark, there were smears of black all over the snow. Blood. A lamentation of swans lay like an unholy sacrifice before Llun's smithy. All their heads were cut off. He understood. Yadovír and Aspidían were not waiting for his answer. He turned around and ran back into the smithy, a red haze before his eyes.

The dog-men must have felt it, because they hung back for the blink of an eye. It was enough. Llun crashed onto them like a wave onto a cliff, and they scattered before him. One swing of the war hammer, and two came down with crushed heads. One tried to lunge under Llun's attack, but Llun had a knife in his left hand, and he plunged it into the man's arm before he could reach his body. With the back hand of his hammer-arm, he crushed the man's shoulder into his backbone. The man screamed.

Only one left.

The last one turned and ran away. Llun put his hammer on the ground and took the knife in his right hand. Balancing it on his fingers, he felt for the center of heaviness, remembering his occasional training from the old days, when he had forged for the warrior seminary. Then he flipped it forward. It landed in the man's neck. He fell, spluttering.

Llun picked up his hammer and rushed toward the nearest of the new roads.

Once in his life, Llun had seen a beehive overturned by a bear. It had been in an outlying village near Vasyllia, where his favorite great-aunt lived with her woodsman husband. The bees, normally sleepy and gentle, had frenzied into a mass of death-dealers that could no longer distinguish their caretaker from a marauding bear. After the bear was done, his aunt had come out —wearing chainmail for good measure. For the first five minutes, they had swarmed her as though she were the bear's consort. Only her stillness and her crooning song had eventually calmed them and allowed his uncle to begin the work of rebuilding the hives.

But she was not here in Vasyllia now to calm the masses that roiled in the streets of the first reach.

Madness seemed to have taken over. It was too dark to make out much except that everyone seemed to be attacking everyone. In brief snatches of focus, Llun saw what looked like Gumiren warriors, judging by their kaftans and silk-sashed caps, attacking and hacking and burning everywhere they went. But there was something wrong about them. Then he heard it. They were speaking Vasylli to each other.

Without another thought, Llun plunged into the swarm, brandishing his war hammer over his head and screaming at the top of his lungs. To his own surprise, he remembered how to use it. It had only been a few lessons with Elder Pahomy of the warrior seminary, years ago now. But he had taken to the weapon like a babe to its mother's teat.

The false Gumiren had not expected any serious resistance. That was clear enough by how they fled from Llun's wrath. But he was fast, in spite of his size. And some kind of war-madness was on him. He had heard a name for it: the war-wind. It was said to make dark gods of men. Well, perhaps Mirodara was right. It was far better to die like this than to continue merely existing in the Vasyllia of the Raven.

The false Gumiren were like sheaves of wheat, and he was the scythe. At fourteen, he lost count of the ones who fell under his war hammer. Before he knew it, the swarming had stopped. Everything was silent, save for the lingering ringing in his ears. Then the sounds of the after-battle began. The crying and the wailing. The wounded. The beloved of the wounded. The war-wind still blew within him. He could not stay here, could not bear to listen to the groans of the weak and fallen.

He ran on, toward the second reach. The Nebesti refugee camps were on fire. Mounted figures rode back and forth, black and demonic against the dancing flames, screaming and whooping. These were not Gumiren. The flopping sacks on their belts —no, they were dogs' heads—revealed them to be warriors of the Consistory. What was going on? Who was attacking whom? Why?

Suddenly, a wave of armed people—they were not warriors, for there were women and children among them—encircled the mounted Consistory men. Banners fluttered among this rag-tag army. In the smoke, it was difficult to make out much, but then the firelight exploded as a tent collapsed, and Llun saw Sirin and other High Beings embroidered on the banners. These were the Sons of the Swan.

His war-wind fled at their sight. So many of them were children! What were they hoping to achieve? Was all this madness of their doing? Is *this* what Mirodara meant when she said that everything was going to change?

Llun was frozen in place, torn between a desire to run and save Mirodara and a gut-deep need to see what was happening in the third reach. Something was going on. Something vital. His hammer could prove important here. But he needed to be near the palace. At the center of everything. He needed to *know*.

With a groan, he wrenched himself away from the sight of the child-army. Running past the Raven's totem, he found time to spit at it. No Gumiren stood guarding it. If he had time, he would have defiled it properly. But no time. Up the gravel roads he ran, the pebbles barely holding him up as he flew with unnatural speed for his bulk. Blasts of fire seemed to be everywhere, exploding even out of bare earth. Then, the rains came. Smoke belched up in black, choking billows. Llun lost all sense of direction, but continued to push upward. Bloodied people ran past him, down into the first reach. Screams burst from in front of him, then behind him, then from the left. Then the screaming was *above* him. He stopped, completely lost, his head spinning, his throat raw from the smoke. He coughed, and it seemed his coughing was adding to the smoke choking everything around them.

The rain fell again in gusting sheets. Then the wind, a gale from the mountain. Everything cleared in Llun's vision suddenly, and he couldn't understand where to look to get his bearing. He fell on the ground, thinking it was the sky.

"There! The smith. Over there!" Vasylli voices. In seconds, black figures surrounded Llun. Dog-men. Llun growled.

"Take care. He's taken many already." The voice was unfamiliar, but unmistakably of the Consistory. It had an emotionless quality about it. Nothing personal, it said. We have to kill you, because it is our business to kill you. Llun raised himself with difficulty, his head still spinning. He tried to orient himself by the tallest tower of the palace, which was directly ahead of him.

He froze. Something was hanging from the turret. A bloody and battered body, hanging on a rope attached to its neck.

Oh, by the Heights. That's... Yadovír!

Something struck him in the back, and searing pain spread across his shoulder blades, hot and prickly. Then something hit his head. Blackness.

∾

Water splashed over his face. For a moment, he couldn't breathe. Then he woke up.

Llun was strapped to some sort of metal post, tied down with both chains and leather. He couldn't move anything except his head. His back tingled with nagging pain that seemed to slowly bore into his backbone. The water splashed over his face again, and he gagged.

"Enough!" he bellowed when he managed to shake the water out his mouth and face. Three dog-men surrounded him, swords drawn and pointed at him. Beyond them, Llun saw darkness. The only light in the dim space came from a table directly ahead of Llun. A single candle, barely illumining the cave-like interior. Three thin, weasel-faced men with salt-and-pepper beards sat there. They were second-reacher, merchant class, judging by their mien and the luxurious fur ringing their felt hats. The hats were red. But the rest of their clothing was black. Black kaftan, black shirts of rippling silk, black vests with silver buckles. Very fancy. One of them, the central one, had dead eyes that latched on Llun's face like a leech on an exposed leg.

"You are Smith Llun, yes? Brother of the traitor Dashun?"

"Hrrmph." Llun's mouth was caked with something sticky. Probably blood. Though his tongue was too swollen to taste it. "Brother-in-law."

"Ah, yes. How stupid of me. Brother of the traitor Vatrina. Even better."

"Worse, you mean," said Llun, under his breath. He had the absurd desire to antagonize that man. To really annoy him.

"Yes, I do," said the man, without expression. "Smith Llun, do you understand why you are here?"

"I may have killed some fifteen of your fellow dog-men."

The man looked down at a parchment before him, as though he had not heard the insult. Then he leaned over to another of the dead-faced inquisitors. None of the three, he now saw, had any expression at all, just blank faces. Not even boredom.

"Twenty-two, by our last count. So, you admit to this treachery and murder of your fellow citizens."

Llun laughed. One of the guards slashed his face with a knife. It left a burning gash—not deep enough to cause serious damage, he felt. These men were good at what they did.

"I do no such thing. I charge you, dog-men of the Consistory, collaborators to the invaders, of treachery and murder. I charge you with impersonating Gumiren to start riots in Vasyllia. I charge you with instigation of violence against your own people and against your unlawfully placed ruler. I—"

This time, the guard punched him with the pommel of his sword in his gut. It was studded with blunt nails. Llun couldn't breathe for a minute, and when he coughed, his stomach lurched in a way that suggested something may have been torn.

"No matter. Your admission is not necessary. Are we in agreement, then?" He turned to one dead-faced inquisitor, then the other. They both nodded, and continued to stare into empty space ahead of them.

"Smith Llun, you are found guilty of conspiring against the state and the person of Yadovír, the Mouth of our Great Father. Your sentencing will be held at a later date."

He waved at the guards, as though he were waving off a mosquito. One of the guards put a bag on Llun's head. It smelled rank. He saw nothing, but suddenly the ground was the ceiling, and his hands were his feet, and...

I have always been fascinated by the effect of pain. Not that I found any particular pleasure in dealing pain. No, that sort of fetish is base. Not worthy of an artist. Rather, I explore how the subject's mind and body twist and mold themselves in incredible ways in response to pain. I have also found ways to control that twisting and molding, to make the subject into something that I can use. That is the true art. To create, as the commons call him, a dog-man. The perfect perpetrator of justice, for he has no conscience of his own. Only the need, bone-deep, to be found worthy in the eyes of his handler.

From the personal notebooks of Aspidían, Grand Inquisitor of the Consistory

CHAPTER 5
A DEAL WITH THE DOG-MAN

L lun awoke. His head throbbed as though separated from his body. He couldn't understand his body's position. He did not feel his feet. Rather, they were there, but not solidly established. His arms were wedged behind him, and something cold pressed against his face. Slowly, concentrating through the throbbing pain, Llun made out that he hung inside a metal cage, his face leaning against one of the bars. He opened his eyes. Nothing changed. Total blackness.

Something whispered far above him, like a soft wind rushing through a narrow passage. The temperature plunged. Something licked his face. He recoiled in terror and disgust, but it kept licking him, like tens of small, ridged tongues, like a cat's. But that wasn't right. No. It was...was it possible? Snow? But he was inside, he was sure of it.

Soon there was no mistaking it. Snow pelted his face. Gritting his teeth against the pain, Llun managed to yank one of his arms out from behind him. He groped across the chain, trying to understand its shape and make. Then he reached further out with his hand. It met stone. Cold, dry stone. Not weathered. No, he was not outside. Then how could it be snowing?

He shivered. Every shudder of his muscles sent arrows of

pain from the center of his back. Something crunched there, like broken cartilage or a ripped ligament.

The temperature fell again. Now it was ice pelting his face, not snow. Wind howled, just like it did during a blizzard. Was he going mad? No, the cold was very, very real.

Then, an explosion of light and heat burst from above his head. He jerked his head without thinking. It struck the metal grating, and his ears rang.

He sweated, his skin tinging where it was encrusted with ice just seconds ago. It was momentarily pleasant. But the heat kept rising. He forced his eyes open, and through the reddish firelight he saw that he was in a tower with no bottom to be seen. Just above his head was some horrifying kind of chandelier, but the heat from its torches was unbearable. He watched with horrified fascination as the hairs on his arms curled up, thickening into deep black, then smoke rose from them as they singed. The smell was sickening, mixed as it was with his own sweat and something far worse. Something rotten and musty and sickly-sweet.

His skin puckered and twitched. It bubbled. Llun closed his eyes, unwilling to see it through to its end.

The light went out. The darkness was so sudden and complete that Llun thought he had gone blind. Something scraped above him—the sound of metal scraping against metal. Cold wind blew in. Hard, sharp snowflakes followed. On his burnt skin, it felt like fire.

It all happened again—the snow, the wind, the biting cold. Only it was a hundred times worse. Then, just when sleepiness began to pull at his eyelids and he was ready to succumb to it, the strange chandelier returned with its blazing heat. Then again it was replaced with the winter storm inside the tower.

At some point, it all blurred into a monotony of agony. Llun must have lost consciousness for a long time, because when he woke up, he was in the throes of a chest-deep cold with a fever so hot, he could probably fry eggs on his forehead. Everything was hazy, and he was sure he had begun to hallucinate. After all, where did that hole in front of him come from?

It was a monstrous emptiness in the stone wall. The sight outside it was so elaborate a deception that Llun decided it must be real.

He had never seen such a sunrise. The clouds were striated like brushstrokes, each layer a deeper red the closer it was to the horizon. The tips of the trees were gilded, while the shadows underneath were a rich nightshade purple. Llun couldn't help himself. He chuckled. This was the perfect torture for an artist. In this place, at this moment, it did not seem absurd that Aspidían had ordered the sunrise especially for Llun. The beauty of it seared his mind, to remain there forever—far more a torment than a relief.

A strange sound reached Llun's ears. It sounded like ... market day. But surely not! Vasyllia wouldn't go back to its daily routine, not after everything that happened. Or ... how long had he been hanging here? At the thought, a hunger so huge it was like a living creature inside his stomach started to claw at him. A long time, then. But still! Had Vasyllia become so depraved that it could just go to market? After all that happened ...

Something cracked inside his head, and he screamed and shook the cage with all the strength he had left. The bars bent, but did not break. All he got for his pains was bloodied fingertips and a headache that felt like two hot pokers pushing his eyes out of his head.

Llun leaned forward, hard. The cage creaked and moved just enough for him to catch a glimpse of the accursed marketplace. It sprawled over the former Temple to Adonais. The ring of red-barks glittered with hundreds of lanterns, but no longer were the lanterns symbols of the flame in the heart, the inner striving for the Heights. Now, they were a convenience that allowed the market to remain open far into the night. This morning, the clearing seethed with brightly-colored dresses of brocade and silk, tall beaver hats, fur-lined mantles sparkling with golden embroidery. The resplendent walking dead.

How dare they! Their own people were being slaughtered in the streets only days ago. By other Vasylli. But still, the market thrives!

Llun's thoughts were interrupted by the sound of footsteps. Many men in a rush. After endless clanking of old keys in even older locks, a sickly light shone far beneath him. Steps echoed through the tower, which Llun now saw was narrow but immensely tall. The figures below him were no bigger than mice. At the head was Aspidían, gesticulating in a manner suggesting, to Llun's surprise, extreme displeasure, directed at a man to his left, apparently the keeper of the tower cells. The man had the air of a dog expecting a beating.

Suddenly, at a strange signal from Aspidían, three of the dogmen behind him grabbed the jailer, who screamed. They dragged him, though he bit them and flailed with his legs so hard Llun was sure his back would break. Another cage lay unused on the ground. They threw him in, so hard it must have broken some of his bones. His screams of defiance quickly changed to supplication, but Aspidían, busy working a rusty winch, ignored him. The chains all clattered at once, then the man's cage began its slow ascent toward the window. To Llun's amazement, his own cage descended at the same time.

Aspidían's face, as it came into focus, was a study in inscrutability. On the one hand, he had the air of a foreman exasperated with his workers, but on the other, something glinted behind his eyes that suggested bestial enjoyment at pain. He smiled.

"Brother Llun!" He raised his hand, as though they were old acquaintances running into each other at a popular market-stand. "You must forgive me. There has been much confusion after the failed coup. I had no idea you were here."

So there had been a failed coup. Or at least, that was what Aspidían wanted Llun to think.

Aspidían led Llun out of the cage with his own hands, and

when his legs failed to support him, he grabbed the huge smith by the waist and forced him to lean on him. Llun was reminded of those snakes from travelers' tales that encircled their prey in a warm embrace before squeezing the life out of them. But he had little strength in his legs, and so he submitted to his torturer.

"Come, my brother," said Aspidían, as cordial as a viper. "Have a drink with me. You look awful."

Llun spat on the ground. But nothing came out. It was like he had been sucked dry.

The long hallways seemed endless. Endless curling staircases, endless rows of black doors. Endless smoking torches jutting out of stone walls that seeped with dark and fetid moisture. The sudden end of the dark was replaced by jagged light. But Llun had grown so accustomed to those changes that he didn't even bother closing his eyes. He just waited for them to adjust.

Aspidían took him to the same room where they had shared mead with Yadovír. Now Llun saw that there were three arched windows looking out directly over the marketplace. He also noticed that the false-commoner hearth had been wiped out of existence. There were new floorboards in the space where it had been. Strange.

Aspidían slumped into one of two extravagant chairs facing the windows and motioned for Llun to do the same. He did, but he nearly fell backward when his muscles failed to hold him. Aspidían laughed.

Between the two chairs stood a short table with a long-necked urn and two squat clay cups.

"I never liked those elaborate goblets," said Aspidían, answering Llun's unspoken question. "And I find clay brings out certain unexpected flavors in the wine."

Llun said nothing, feeling the tension behind Aspidían's words, even through the haze of his burning fever. "Brother Aspidían," whispered Llun. "Who did it? Who killed Yadovír?"

Aspidían turned on him, and for a moment Llun thought

that he was going to bite him like a rabid dog. Breathing like a bellows, Aspidían steadied himself.

"You know who," he said.

"The Gumiren?"

Aspidían nodded. "And not only they. The Sons of the Swan. They colluded with the Gumiren. Can you imagine? After all that talk of evil collaborators and traitors to Vasyllia? They did it themselves!"

"That's not possible." It came out before Llun could stop it.

Aspidían smiled, but it was poisonous. "Oh? Enlighten me then."

"There were Vasylli dressed as Gumiren in the first reach, killing and destroying everything in their path. And..." His head spun, and he had to cover his eyes with shaking hands. "It...it was Consistory men who burned down the Nebesta refugee camp."

Aspidían shook his head and sighed. "So much madness. So much confusion. Everyone pretending to be someone else. We need... we need to purge the filth from Vasyllia. For the last time."

"How will you identify friend from foe?"

"Oh, we have ways." He smiled, probably contemplating some especially subtle form of torture. "Shall I demonstrate?"

Aspidían jumped to the windowsill. Llun was surprised to see that the arches were open to the air with not even a thin layer of parchment against the elements, though how no wind or cold blew in, he couldn't understand. Aspidían whistled and nodded. A drum rolled. Easily visible through the arched windows before them, lines of spear-bearing Consistory men surrounded the market from all sides. The bustling people, without even thinking, all stopped their purchasing, haggling, gossiping and stood still, as though they were hoping that they wouldn't be seen if they didn't move.

"Brother Llun, I know you do not think highly of the new

way of Vasyllia. But I will show you how effective it can be. It is winnowing time."

Llun stood up from his seat, his head spinning for a moment before his body found its place, and put a hand on the arch to better see. His hand was thinner than he remembered, and the sight of caked blood on it confused him. In the haze of the fever, he had almost forgotten the torture. Had it actually happened? He shook his head, trying to clear the mist from his thoughts. The hot pokers behind his eyes prodded him, and he saw stars. He almost fell, but the wall caught him.

Aspidían braced himself against his side of the arch, looking at Llun. He was done with pretense, it seemed, though his posture was casual, even languid. He even seemed faintly bored. Again, Llun had the sense that he was stuck in a dream where the details were terribly clear but made little sense when put together.

"People of Vasyllia!" Somehow, Aspidían's voice echoed through all Vasyllia below them, as though the mountains caught his voice like a child's wooden ball and threw it back and forth for their own amusement. Every face in the crowd craned upward, listening intently. "Please forgive the intrusion into your day of rest and pleasure. After what we have all been through, you deserve it. But we now have clear evidence. Yadovír, the man who is so dear to all of us, who has made the transition to the new order as bearable as possible, was betrayed by his own people. Yes, the Gumiren killed him. But we now know that he was delivered to the Gumiren by those vipers, those hawks wearing dove's tail-feathers. It was all an attempted coup. By the Sons of the Swan."

The crowd seethed as people began to whisper to each other and push each other and gesticulate. From this distance, it looked like an anthill disturbed by the stick of a small boy.

"Yes, my people," he shouted over them, arm outstretched for silence. "I know your anger, your frustration with these cowards, these degenerates, these postulants of a retrograde idea. It is time to winnow them from our ranks. I charge you. If any of you know of a friend, a neighbor, or even a family member who is of the Sons, you must come forward. The doors of the Consistory are at your disposal. Come. Let us cleanse the foulness of the Sons from our Vasyllia!"

He turned back to Llun, his face a careful blank. "As soon as I hear of Mirodara's involvement, I will bring her here before you. You will sit there and watch as I kill her. Slowly. Would you like to hear the details of my process? It is quite...artistic."

Llun's hands shook, and his head spun wildly. He was sure he would faint. With an effort of will, he straightened himself and looked down at Aspidían. Such a small man. He would be able to crush his head with a single hand. Yet he had so much power in him.

"I will be your man, Aspidían. But you must promise not to touch Mirodara."

Aspidían looked away from Llun, a slight smile playing at the edges of his lips. Swift as an adder, he backhanded Llun across the face. Hot, wet blood spurted. He had struck him on the place where the dog-man had sliced him during his mock trial. Llun looked at the blood on his hands, and could no longer support his own weight. He fell on his knees, the sobs racking his stomach. He released them, and a blubbering groan came out of his mouth. He hardly recognized it.

"Don't imagine you can haggle with me, vermin. You will do what I say."

Llun breathed deep. His heart slowly calmed, and he looked up at Aspidían. Deep inside, there was still something left of his strength. He shook his head.

"No, Brother Aspidían. You let too much slip. I don't know why, but you need me. And I will kill myself before I help you, if you so much as scratch Mirodara."

Aspidían held his gaze for an endless minute. Then he collapsed into hearty, chesty laughter.

"Oh, Llun! I'm so glad I met you. It's impossible to be bored with you around."

He snapped his fingers, and two dog-men appeared. They picked Llun up and carried him back the same way they had come.

"No," whispered Llun.

"Oh, yes," said one of the guards, flashing his eyebrows up and down at his companion.

They took Llun back to his cage.

I do not know if this letter will ever reach you, my beloved. I know that you are doing everything you can to come back to me. And I know that the forces arrayed against you must be strong indeed. But Voran, my love, I do not know how much longer I can hold on. I lost my body on the night of the Fall. I can hardly feel it any more. I fear my mind will be next. They say that you have become a Healer. Come to me, my love. Heal me. I need you.

From an unsent letter found in the apartments of Darina Sabíana of Vasyllia

CHAPTER 6

THE DARINA OF VASYLLIA

The first night, the cycle of cold and hot repeated five times. The second night, the cycle repeated six times. By the fifth day, Llun had trouble distinguishing day from night. It may have been a month, it may have been a year. The fever in his body reached some kind of critical point, and there was a period when Llun remembered nothing. He came back to consciousness with a strange sensation of being that he had never before experienced. He felt every fiber of his body separately. He moved individual muscles with a clear understanding of where they began and ended and how they worked. At the same time, every breath was an unbearable agony. It was as if there were two of him.

"There's more to this than mere torture, you know," she said. "There's a foul magic at work here. Not something I understand. But I've seen it at work in others already. They're preparing you. Reforging you, if you like. To be able to withstand the horrors that you will perpetrate on others. And, possibly, for something even worse."

Where did she come from? And how did he suddenly get from his cage to this garret? It looked like an unused attic room, the kind where all the unnecessary bric-a-brac of a great house was placed in piles that were once orderly, but had long ceased to be so. Immense mounds of fabric, bits of metal, broken chairs. But then there was the wooden throne, its every inch carved into shapes of Sirin and wolves and giants and vila that came out of the wood like ripples on water. It was illumined with a dappled fire-light that...yes, it was fragrant. Like roses.

"I will not be like them," he said to the figure on the throne, whom he could not quite see, though he didn't understand why.

"No, I don't believe you will. But there will be a price to pay."

Something about the voice enchanted Llun. It awoke forgotten images of sharp mountain peaks and waterfalls at dawn, images associated with a childhood longing that flared in his heart whenever he listened to his mother sing a ballad of Old Vasyllia.

"I will gladly pay the price of my life," said Llun.

"You do not know what you are saying," said the figure. She shifted in the throne, and the light also changed, so that he could see her more clearly. She was a young, dark-haired woman in chainmail, a heavy wolf fur draping her shoulders. Across her chest flew a black swan embroidered on a snow-white field. Her expression was still, but joyful. It was almost as though she were laughing at Llun, except her eyes were so old, deep as a lake with no visible bottom, that Llun was certain she was incapable of mocking others.

"What if you did give them the gift of your life to save your niece? Mirodara, was it? You would be able to bear it, perhaps, but only because you knew you would die eventually. At some point, all the pain will end. Perhaps you even keep suicide in the back of your mind as an extreme measure."

She sighed and shook her head. Her hair shone in the fire-light, mesmerizing Llun with the play of dark red and brown and even purple tints.

"But you don't understand what the Raven is. His eternal quest is for endless life. And if he does find the source of endless life, whether in the form of Living Water or in some other unknown form, then imagine what they can do to their dog-men. Given a few centuries of constant atrocities, a few centuries for the mind to hide their atrocities under a mental scar, they will be capable of any evil. Not just capable, but confirmed in it. Any internal change will become impossible. They will not think twice about murder, rape, torture. They will no longer be men."

"Why are you telling me this? And who are you?"

"Can you not guess who I am?" She smiled mischievously, patting the black swan on her chest with her forefinger, with an expression that said, "Can it be any more obvious?"

"You are Darina Sabíana? But they say you are bed-ridden. Unable to move."

"Yes, that is all true," she said, faintly annoyed, "but you are also in a cage, are you not? And yet you stand here with me."

Llun opened his mouth to retort, but found nothing to say.

"Have you never wondered," she said, "why your name is Llun?"

The name was a rare one, it was true. "I always thought my mother wanted to be unique."

Sabíana rolled her eyes. "Not much imagination, for an artist. No. Have you never considered the importance of names before? Why, for example, there are so few Cassíans and so many Lassars in Vasyllia?"

"Oh," he understood immediately. "It's the old superstition. You need to give your child the name of a person who was successful in life. For good luck. Name a child after a martyr, and ..." He chuckled significantly.

"No, no, no," she waved her hands in frustration. "That's the ... No ... There is something profoundly important about naming. It's not a matter of luck. The name does, in some ineffable way, reflect a person's place in the Universal Harmony. Have you never wondered why in some of the Old Tales, you have different characters with the same name living in vastly different circumstances, yet in all of them, the same events keep happening? It's not an accidental pattern. It's part of the fabric of the creation."

"But Llun. He was a mad prophet, wasn't he? His writings in the *Sayings* are incredibly arcane. More interpretations of his prophecies exist than the prophecies themselves. What does that say about me and my name?"

"Llun wrote of a terribly important event. A time of blood, when the dead would walk as though living, but with no souls to speak of. He said that he, Llun himself, would bring this time about as a punishment for Vasyllia's iniquity. But..."

"Oh, you mean he could have meant that I am the Llun that will bring divine retribution? How?"

"I cannot say for certain. But Aspidían has been studying Llun's prophecies for years. He even comes to me in my bed of misery to speak of it. He finds no one else who believes him. But he seems to think that a smith is necessary. You are to make something. Something rather banal, I think. But with unexpected uses."

Hardly helpful. "Why are you telling me all this, my lady?"

"It's the only thing I have left, you see," she said. "And it is why I linger here in Vasyllia. I am given to help those who are needed at Vasyllia's sticking points. Yours is coming. You may have to make the most difficult choice of all. To abandon everything. Not only your own life, not only your own death, but even Mirodara."

"No. That I will not do."

"And yet, the alternative will be far worse than you can imagine."

"I will not!"

The pain in his back grew and arched and exploded into stars that danced before his eyes, before they pulled him back underneath into the darkness. He felt turned inside out, and once again his legs were clamped in place, his arms hanging useless outside the cage that was too small for him. He closed his eyes and tried to sleep.

And I, Llun of Vasyllia, will bring down the retribution of the Heights on fallen Vasyllia. The stars shall weep blood, the immortal one shall hold the lifeblood of the worlds in the palm of his hand, and the Realms themselves will hold their breath for utter terror. But in that day, the truth will become known at last. And the fire-born will brave the seventh baptism to demand vengeance from the Throne of the Most High himself.

From "The Prophecy of Llun"
(The Sayings, Book XXIII, 10:3-6)

CHAPTER 7
THE CHOICE

When Llun came to himself, he was no longer in the cage, but in a simple prison cell. He lay on a straw pallet on a wooden ledge. A pitcher of water was at his feet. He attacked the pitcher, spilling much of the contents on the ground in his haste. His hands shook, and he was unable to stop them. His hands...they were blackened with soot, thin and brittle-looking. How would he ever again manage to create anything with his hands? Why did they do this to him, if they wanted him to become the exclusive smith of the Consistory? Or had they now abandoned all that?

Still, despite his shaking hands, he felt clear-headed for the first time since the ordeal began. He groped his chest and arms, trying to see how much muscle mass he had lost. It was not as bad as he thought. About as much as he would have expected after not eating for a week. No, they hadn't been torturing him for months or years, then. Only days.

It was then that he realized that, outside, some sort of commotion had been going on ever since he had woken up. He listened, trying to understand. Lots of pushing and jostling, by the sound of it. Scraping metal. Gumiren voices, angry, yet without that note of defiance that usually characterized their speech. These voices sounded...yes, frightened.

So, the pogroms have begun, then.

He was too tired to feel any emotion accompanying that thought.

For the next few days, he was brought heaping plates of chicken and boar meat. It was unseasoned and not very well made, but these were the tastiest meals of Llun's life. Almost in the space of hours, he began to regain his strength. His hands stopped shaking. He found the courage to try to scratch off the scorch marks on his skin. All that came off was a layer of dead skin. Underneath, everything was smooth, almost baby-like. Strange for a man whose skin was more like leather after a lifetime at the forge. But it would harden again, soon enough.

A few days later, Aspidían himself came in the morning, bearing a tray of roasted ribs. Even from a distance, Llun smelled the rosemary. This was a king's meal, not a prisoner's. Behind Aspidían came a host of servants bearing trestles, stands, plates, crockery, spices, and wine. Urns and urns of wine. Llun's mouth watered at the sight, even at the clinking of the cups on the makeshift trestles.

"What are you doing?" asked Llun, his voice hardly more than a croak.

"Your last meal," said Aspidían, smiling. When Llun's jaw clenched, Aspidían laughed. "Your face! Even after all we've put you through, you're still as innocent as a babe in swaddling clothes."

Llun didn't know whether to laugh or cry. Aspidían poured wine for them both. It was blood-red, almost viscous.

"I wasn't lying when I said it was your last meal. It is. From this moment, you will be something else. It will be your choice, what you will be. But not Llun the smith of the former first reach of Vasyllia." He raised his cup. "To the new order."

Llun hesitated a moment, then drank. There was something different about this wine. It burned him on the inside. Llun suspected that there was more than just wine there. But Aspidían drank it with Llun, so it was not poison. At least, not the kind that kills.

"New order, you say?" croaked Llun. "One cleansed of both the Gumiren and the Sons of the Swan?"

"Oh yes," said Aspidían. "You would not believe how willing our Vasylli were to rat out the Sons. So many traitors in our midst!"

"You do realize that people will say anything to keep themselves from being implicated. It proves nothing."

"Yes, yes. But that is well and good. It doesn't matter who remains in the new Vasyllia, really. As long as they understand the new rules. As long as they are the ones who will resist external influence to the last drop of their blood. As for the Gumiren, we've killed most of them already. The Ghan escaped with a small band of his elite warriors, but they have nowhere to go. They'll be found in the mountains soon enough. If not, they'll have a surprise waiting for them at the border with Nebesta." He chuckled. The expression on his face left no doubt that whatever it was, it would be painful and probably fatal.

He snapped his fingers, and the servants began slicing the ribs apart. The meat practically fell off the bone. Llun's hands shook again, and it took all the will he had left not to attack the food. Aspidían watched him the whole time and seemed pleased with what he saw. Finally, all the ribs were separated and placed in a pile in the middle of the table. A servant tossed herbs over it, and another poured sauce that smelled strongly of onion and beer.

Aspidían inhaled deeply, eyes closed in pleasure. He sat there, savoring the smell, for what seemed an eternity.

Llun could wait no longer. "Tell me what I want to know," he said. He knew that he risked losing this meal, possibly the most elaborate and well-made meal of his life. He didn't care anymore.

Aspidían inclined his head and smirked. "Yes, Mirodara was turned in. I've kept her safe, for now. I was waiting to see how you'd do in your ordeal. And you did surprisingly well, considering the ordeal lasted almost two weeks. Do you know how many postulates to the Consistory survive it? Less than half."

"You risked losing your exclusive smith?" Llun said, with a hint of mockery.

"Yes." Aspidían became deadly serious. "Enough games, Llun. The Great Father needs you for a frightfully important work. I know you are squeamish about serving him, but you were never a particularly devout member of the cult of Adonais. You weren't much of anything, really. But we live in a time where half measures have no place. I think you know that now, and not merely with your mind."

Llun nodded. His body would never forget the lesson.

"You are more important than you know, Llun." Aspidían pulled out his table knife and speared three ribs through, then dropped them on Llun's side of the table. "Eat, O important one."

Llun did. Somehow, he managed not to transform into a wolf on the spot, but ate with admirable restraint. Or so it seemed to him. Aspidían shook his head with a smile, again in his faintly amused persona.

"Brother Llun, have you ever read the prophecies of your namesake?"

So she had been real. The warrior-Darina who spoke to him from her throne.

"Of course ... when I was a child. Everyone reads *The Sayings* at least once."

"Ah ... you have not *read* them, then. Have you ever heard the idea that names are not accidental? That when one takes on the name of another, especially an illustrious name, he takes up some of the qualities of his namesake?"

"I have not given it much thought, to be honest."

"Well, you would not be the first. But your name. What a name! A rare one. And with good reason. 'The Prophecies of Llun' is the strangest book in *The Sayings*. So many contradictory interpretations. So many phrases with no apparent meaning. Until now."

Llun's back straightened as he listened, unwittingly enchanted by Aspidían's voice. The pain was there, but now no more than an ache. Amazing. Sabíana was right about the body's ability to heal itself. Or was it perhaps something in the wine? Something with the appearance of goodness, but actually dangerous?

"There is a series of images that keeps popping up," continued Aspidían. "Most of them involve fire and a night full of stars in the constellation of the sword. The stars begin to weep. Then the tears turn to blood. By themselves, these images make little sense. But there is a mathematical precision to the prophecies. Certain images appear at regular intervals. Every seven verses, every twelve verses, and every four chapters, these central images repeat. I won't bore you with the calculation, but I have managed to make a cipher of the prophecies. They speak of a moment in Vasyllia's history when the lifeblood of the worlds will come into the hands of an 'immortal one.' At that time, the key to life and death will be revealed, and the dead will walk as though alive."

"*As though* alive? Animate corpses walking around Vasyllia? Sounds horrifying." He thought of the people in the market and realized that part of the prophecy may have already come true. They were no better than animate corpses.

"I do not jest, Llun. I am speaking of something monumental." His eyes widened, his eyebrows shot up, and he spoke in hushed, awed tones. "I have the ear of the Great Father. He has helped me to understand the true meaning of everything that has happened. All the suffering Vasyllia's been through. All the troubles. Nothing more than a cleansing. A time of ordeal. We are about to embark on a new age for Vasyllia. One unmatched in glory in the history of the world. Man will not lord it over man. Everyone will be equal. Opportunities to rise in the world will be given to all. Every person may choose what he or she would like to be. And the might of Vasyllia will become legendary. Then we will be a beacon, a city on a hill, truly. Other nations will seek alliance with us, and we can choose with whom to associate. No more need to pander after the pitiful Nebesti or worse, the Karila.

"At the heart of this new world will be the ultimate gift. Eternal life. Even now, the Raven is at the cusp of finding it. But it will only be given to the chosen. Only to the men of the Raven. They will live for all time."

Sabíana's warning about an eternity of atrocity rang in Llun's ears like a bell. Truly, she was right. If the dog-men had millennia to live, they would be no different than changers or any other evil Power.

And yet...

"Brother Aspidían. I hear you. I am moved by your words. But I am a simple man, not given to theorizing. Tell me, simply, how I am to help in this new age of Vasyllia?"

"You will be one of the Consistory. But not yet. After a time. First, a test. There is a trinket that the Great Father would have you make for him. A simple thing, really. A metal flask that a man can wear on his hip. To hold wine or mead or water, even."

Llun was taken aback. He had expected something elaborate. But a flask? And a metal one, to boot? He had never seen such a thing. Why would anyone want to drink water from a metal flask? What was wrong with leather skins?

"Is there any design the...um...Great Father would prefer? Any details he would like included?"

"He wants you to...be possessed by your inspiration."

Again, Llun shuddered at the use of that particular word. It tainted his enjoyment of the rest of that meal. It didn't help that though his mind registered how superior the cooking was, his heart ached with worry for Mirodara and fear for what he would have to do. Aspidían was content to allow Llun his silence, though he talked the entire time. Llun had only a faint recollection of what he spoke about, but it left a sour taste in Llun's mouth.

To Llun's surprise, Aspidían led him through the Consistory back to the outer courtyard of the palace.

He's not letting me go home, is he?

At the gates, Aspidían embraced Llun and hugged him warmly. Llun stiffened, not sure whether to be afraid or uncomfortable.

"I am giving you this day and night as a gift," said the dogman. "For you and Mirodara. Use it well. For both your sakes, help her understand the way that is best for all."

It has been the source of some debate—where did the essence of the Raven go when Yadovír was killed? Some survivors of the wars for Vasyllia insist that, a few nights after the death of Yadovír, they saw the presence of the Raven hovering about a smithy in the first reach. Impossible to confirm now, of course, since that smithy no longer stands...

From "A New History of the Covenant" by Dar-in-Exile
Mirnían II

CHAPTER 8
THE CREATION

Mirodara lay curled in a ball on the floor of his back room. She did not budge at his call. She shrank from his touch on her shoulder.

"What did they do to you?" he asked, shaking with the suppressed desire to kill everyone who would dare to so much as lay a hand on her.

She uncurled slowly, like a flower opening over the course of a long morning. Her eyes were hollow. Not a sign of tears on her face. Just horror lurking behind her eyes, like a parasite that had invaded her body. She would not look him in the eyes. The closest she managed to get was somewhere near his left eyebrow. He waited for her to sit up, giving her what he hoped was enough space to feel safe, without the distance he feared would clam her up even more. He wanted to enfold her in his arms, to hide her in his bulk, to never let anyone else see her.

"Not much," she said, but it sounded like she had forgotten how to speak. Her own face looked surprised at the sound of her voice. "It's what they did to the others. They made me watch." Her face turned green, and her hands went up to her mouth as she retched. But nothing came out. She dry heaved for almost a minute.

Llun went outside to the well and pulled out a bucketful of water. He nearly threw it on her head in his haste and in his desire to make her better. She had to calm him down by taking his lone wooden cup and dipping it in the cold water. Her eyes closed at the pleasure of the water.

"You must have some bread. I have a little. I think..."

His bread box was nearly empty, and what was there may have been a feast for the mice in the last few weeks, judging by the suspicious looking crumbs in the left corner. Sighing out his exasperation, he took his table knife out of its sheath on his belt —he still couldn't believe the dog-men had given it back to him —and cut a thin outside layer off the crusty, black rye bread. Without much hope, he looked in the apple basket for last year's shriveled apples, few of which had survived the winter. He was shocked to find one tiny, shriveled, but bright red apple hiding in the far corner. He picked it up. It smelled like autumn.

Mirodara took both the bread and the apple and looked at them for a long moment, not understanding what they were, or what she was supposed to do with them. That, more than anything else, cut his heart. How could he go through with it? They'd already damaged Mirodara, possibly beyond repair. She was not strong enough to survive what was coming.

But the food gave her obvious strength. Her breathing slowed and deepened, and a spot of warmth touched her cheeks, though they were still far from a good color. It was as though the blush of healthfulness had gingerly approached her cheek, had even tried to warm it, but ultimately scurried away like a skittish deer. Still, she looked much better for the food and water.

"Why?" she asked as he brought her tea, the last of his precious hoard, probably never to be replenished now.

"Why what, my cub?"

"Why are you and I here, now, speaking to each other? Is this a test? Are they waiting outside, waiting for you to lull me into a sense of security, so I can let slip some vital piece of information about the Sons of the Swan?"

She looked at him with such a strange expression—anger, distrust, defiance, exhaustion. And yet, they had not stamped out the hope, deep within her eyes, no more than a fading ember.

"It is a sort of test, I think," he said. "But not the one you think. This is the last chance you and I have to lead a normal life before everything changes. I am to become one of them. To save your life. And maybe even to save your death."

She stiffened. "Oh, Heights! Has the Raven found it, then? His immortality?"

"No, not that I can tell. But I think he is close. The Consistory wants me to make something for him. I don't understand it, not quite. Aspidían did a very bad job trying to make it sound unimportant. But what the Raven would want with a metal flask, I haven't the faintest idea."

Mirodara's eyebrows gathered in confusion. "That's...unexpected. One of the Sons was deep inside the Consistory, and before the last purge, he managed to find out that the Raven is burrowing *inside* Vasyllia. Inside the mountain, searching for some elixir, like the Living Water, but possibly something else entirely. I know, bad information. It's the best we have."

"It's clearly important. Maybe the flask is intended to hold this elixir. But wouldn't it have to be a magical artifact then, to hold a thing of power?"

"Perhaps you have magical powers you weren't aware of."

It was a joke, though she barely smiled as she said it. It made Llun smile and nearly exclaim in joy.

"Llun, you must do what you think is right. But let me say one thing. I don't know why, but I think that this object will be your last as a smith. Your work is too beautiful to be allowed by the Raven. And I think that you need to be very careful when you make it. It's going to be not a battle, but a war."

He knew what she meant. Every *thing* he made was made with pain, in a process of battle with himself and with forces outside himself that tried to stop him—tiredness, lack of inspiration, a sense that he was incapable of creating beauty. Only after it was complete did the sense of synthesis, the joy intertwined with intense grief, come flooding over him, threatening to overwhelm him. In that moment, he and the Heights were one, until once again the hunger for creation overtook him, and the process began anew.

If, instead of the usual, natural antagonists, the Raven and his dark Powers interfered with his work or tried to subvert it to their own desires, the struggle would be a hundred times more intense. It might even kill him.

But what better way to die, than in the creation of a perfect piece that would never, not over his dead body, belong to them? After all, nothing created through the mediation of the Heights would ever be corrupted. It would simply be. And even if they later used it for their own vile ends, its beauty would be a thorn in their side, a reminder of their eventual failure and end. For nothing evil can last forever, not unless it were already the Unmaking of the world.

"Yes, Mirodara. You will have to help me. There will be times when I will want to stop. Or when my creation will try to wrest itself from my hands. Be my cold water. Be my conscience."

She smiled, and the ember of hope in her eyes lit up.

"Our last hurrah. Yes. It will be glorious."

"I must do it in my forge. And I need Mirodara with me."

Aspidían had come to the first reach with a full honor guard, and he looked a little offended at being thus greeted. But that quickly passed, as understanding crept in. Again, Aspidían surprised Llun. He had expected at least something of a fight.

"I understand," said Aspidían. He looked at Llun, his gaze slowly boring into him as though he were pushing a knife into his eye, waiting for it to come out the other end. He dismissed the guards with a wave of the hand, still looking at Llun.

"Only know this. This is a concession. My final one. After you join us, you will not come back here. In fact, I intend to destroy this smithy. I know about the foulness that you perpetrated here. Those decorative shields. I did not see it at first. But later, after the benefit of some...external aid," for a moment, the mask slipped, and Aspidían's pain shone in his eyes. Was the inquisitor the recipient of the tender mercies of the torturer himself? "I recognized them for what they were. I should take both hands from you for that. And both eyes for good measure."

"I understand you, Brother Aspidían."

He met the inquisitor's gaze. It was terrifying, but already Llun felt the beginning of the inspiration. The process of creation. He could not be gainsaid by anyone when in this state. Aspidían began to smile his adder's smile, but he stopped in midsmirk. His eyes softened, and a face Llun had yet to see manifested itself. It was terrifyingly, heartbreakingly sad.

"Brother Llun. It is my great regret that we did not know one another before ..." He choked on what he almost said, before his eyes filmed over with their usual expression of assumed boredom. He turned and followed the honor guard back to the Consistory.

For a moment, Llun watched in wonder. Was this last, sincerest version of Aspidían the greatest lie of all?

But the forge called to him like a lover after a long absence. And Mirodara's gaze was burning swirls into his back.

"I'm ready," he said.

"I don't think you are," she said, but she was deadly serious.

A shudder ran up his spine. She was right.

Llun took the piece of iron like a mother taking her child from the midwife. Llun folded the iron gently into a thick block. He cut the block into two billets and placed the two halves on top of each other, with the grains perpendicular to each other. Then, he forged it into a thin sheet, so thin, he was afraid it would crack in multiple places at the smallest stress. But it held.

As soon as the sheet was ready to be shaped, it began. The

heaviness in his mind. Usually it was no more than a kind of fog that pushed him to stop, to lay down his tools to wait for a better moment, when his heart would be more into the process. But this time, it was like a voice in his head.

You are weak. Why do you labor? You know that it can never be appreciated for what it truly is. It is going to be twisted out of shape and out of its intention. Better give it up. Come what may.

He was already sweating, but now it poured like rain down his body. His breathing hurried, and the heat on his face was more than just the forge.

"You don't matter," said Mirodara. "*You* don't matter. This thing you make. It matters more than you or I or my mother or anyone else. It may be the last thing of beauty created in Vasyllia."

He breathed a sigh of relief as the enthusiasm caught at the wave of his shame. He began to shape the iron around a rounded wooden block. It felt like butter in his hands, supple and easy. So easy. He could do anything he wanted with this. Would he be remembered for this creation? Would Vasyllia sing the praises of Llun the smith after this final, wondrous thing he made?

A flask?

Truly, an insignificant, pitiful thing to make as one's swan song. Why not change it? He could use this metal to make a weapon so fine, so strong, that it would make even the dullest swordsman brilliant. Why not? Surely such a gift would be acceptable to the Great Father.

Great Father? Have you gone mad?

Something chuckled behind them.

"Don't look," said Mirodara, her voice shaking. "He wants you, Llun. Not as a smith. They've been lying to you the whole time. He doesn't want your flask. He wants *you* as his..." Her voice squelched, like someone were holding a wet towel over her mouth and throttling her by the neck at the same time. Llun nearly turned around. Something kept him firmly in place, working the sheet around the mold.

The presence in the room was unmistakable, its malice so palpable it was akin to a smell of something rotten, like old eggs or a week-old corpse. And yet, there was a kind of energy in that presence. It fueled Llun's manic activity. His hands worked faster than they ever had before, with as much, or more, control than he had had since his early days. Already he saw the decorations of iron he would place on the flask, fine as embroidery.

No! Not for him. Not ever!

There were two Lluns in that room. One was already finished with the creation of the flask—a marvelous thing that sparkled even in darkness, that was light as a feather but virtually unbreakable. A perfect receptacle for an elixir of power. The other Llun was still in his human body, sweating, aching, laboring over the sheet, which every second threatened to break apart into splinters of iron. This Llun was tired. He wanted to give up. The other Llun, the one in his mind—how he wanted to be him already! To rush past the drudgery of the work. To stand at the completed stage, the state of synthesis, to feel the joy of it.

"*I can give it to you,*" said the presence in his mind, "*all you have to do is desire it with every fiber of your being.*"

"Is beauty without suffering possible?" asked a new voice, strong and regal. Sabíana stood before him, half-insubstantial, her eyes dancing in the shower of sparks Llun sent up with each blow of his hammer. "Is it even preferable? You are the last true artist in Vasyllia, Llun. Not because of some talent given by the Heights. You are the last in the tradition of the old masters. The ones who understood that the secret of beauty is pain. Only through birthgiving can the miracle be brought forth."

The presence in his mind laughed. "*Yes. Listen to the woman. She is a pitiful creature, chained to her bed. I offer you the way of fulfillment. It is also the path to power. Never again will you be subject to the whims of the Consistory. You will rule them.*"

"You have no power here, foul thing," Sabíana cried. "This is a place protected by me. It is given to me from above, this protection for my chosen few."

Again, the laughter, only now directed at her. *"And what if I told you that everything you think you know about your precious Power, your Adonais, is a lie? What if I told you that your entire existence is a mistake, but one that is mercifully coming to its end? What would you say to that, eh?"*

Sabíana's eyes filled with tears and she shimmered for a moment, then faded.

"You see? She cannot protect you. Only you can protect yourself. And Mirodara as well. Save her from what the Consistory will do. Become the Consistory.*"*

Llun breathed deeply and closed his eyes. He stilled his breathing and focused on the beating of his heart. It began to slow. He waited until the beats were regular and unhurried. He breathed again and smiled. Everything hurt. His mind, his body. Everything. And he loved it. He would have it no other way. He would make this thing. This last thing of beauty.

But not for you. Begone, you foulness. You have no place in the creation of the beautiful.

"Llun? Are you well? What happened?"

Mirodara touched his shoulder.

"Is it...Can I turn around now?" He asked.

"Yes. I think it's over."

Llun turned to look at her. She was unharmed. Only a little pale. He nodded at her and turned back to his work, suddenly sure that the time needed to create this thing properly would not be given them. With a speed he never expected from himself, he created something... remarkable.

He puffed like a bellows after it was done, cradling the thing in his hand like a child. It was a flask, but it did not even look metal. It looked like a dark flower enfolded in leaves at midnight. It was the most beautiful thing Llun had ever seen. And he recognized that it was not *he* who had made it. He was but the instrument.

"Mirodara," he said. "Go. Take it. You are its only hope. It must never fall into the hands of the Raven. Find a way. Leave

Vasyllia. Seek the true Vasylli out there, in the wild. If you find Voran the Healer, tell him to hurry. There may not be a Vasyllia left if we wait much longer."

The doors to the forge flew open. Aspidían stood there, his gaze expectant. It quickly turned to disappointment, then anger, then horror.

"What...? What have you done, Llun? Where is Mirodara?"

"I am ready," said Llun. "I am ready to be a dog-man."

Aspidían gestured, and the guards behind him swarmed in and seized Llun, pulling him out of the smithy on his knees.

"Turn him around," said Aspidían. "Make him watch."

Ten dog-men with torches stood in a semicircle around Aspidían, their eyes red in the fire-light.

"Burn it," said Aspidían. "The whole block."

And it came to pass that the sacrifice was offered, and it was found acceptable by the Most High. And he deigned to bend down from the throne of his greatness to confirm the sacrifice, and to give a final gift. But his words were terrible. Thus saith the Lord, the Most High: "For the last time I grant the fallen a boon, until the fire-born braves the final baptism and stands before me in his transfigured flesh."

From "The Prophecy of Llun"
(The Sayings, Book XXIII, 4:1-4)

CHAPTER 9
THE ESCAPE

Mirodara dropped the flask into the first canvas pack she found lying in a heap of rubble in Llun's smithy. It tied over her shoulder well enough. She hoped it wouldn't look conspicuous in the first reach. She must do everything possible not to attract too much attention to herself on her way out of Vasyllia.

She stopped at a food stand and bought three breads and some dried meat. Enough, she hoped, to get her into Nebesta, where she would try to find some gainful employment while she searched for Voran. She had nothing more concrete than that as far as plans go. Some very reasonable part of her, deep inside her mind, nagged at her that the lack of a plan was no plan at all, but she was too excited by her forthcoming adventure to listen.

Only when she was halfway to her destination—a side gate in Vasyllia's wall that was usually undermanned and filled with merchant wains entering and exiting—did it fully hit her. She would never see Llun again. She sped up her walking, if only to force the hard cobbles in the streets to rattle her out of her desire to sink to the ground and weep like a baby. It was no use, not any more. Yes, she was an orphan, but she had gotten over that (or so she kept telling herself). Now she had no one left. But the world was ending. What difference did it make if there was no one to share it with?

Focusing on the ground before her feet, she almost didn't notice that she was at the gates, even as she joined the line of people leaving. Her good fortune held strong. Several caravans of merchants were lining up to take the shorter, more difficult routes that skirted the mountains and led out to the lands that used to be taboo to the Vasylli. Magical lands with monstrous creatures with many eyes that spun silk out of their own saliva. If the stories were to be believed. Mirodara certainly believed them.

She tried her best to blend into the gaggle of merchants, some even with their families, as they prepared to take a journey that could last them years. What sort of hopes animated them? How did they survive in the new Vasyllia? Were they not also affected by all the madness? Perhaps they did well to leave, hoping beyond hope that things would be different when they returned?

A little boy of two or three saw Mirodara and started making faces at her. She did the same, and he laughed with pleased surprise.

"What's your name?" she asked him quietly.

"Adarin," he said, sheepishly.

"I'm Mirodara," she said. "Do you want to play a game?"

He nodded, eyes sparkling.

"I'm going to hide under your father's wain, under here. But I have to get there without anyone noticing me. You can help me, right?"

"I want to hide with you, too," he said.

"But then we'll both get in trouble, won't we? I'll tell you what. If you help me hide now, I'll let you come down with me for the rest of the trip. I just need to be under there when we pass the gates. Got it?"

Adarin looked dubious, but he obviously wanted to play. He nodded seriously, then started to scream bloody murder. Every adult within earshot was completely absorbed by his screaming. Mirodara slipped under a wain and held on for dear life. As soon as she did, Adarin stopped, as though it were the most normal thing in the world to scream one second, then stop the next. Mirodara had to bite her lip to keep from laughing aloud.

Just as they approached the gates, Mirodara heard the stomp of booted feet. Many booted feet.

"Stop the wains, stop the wains!" Someone called from behind.

"What's the matter, sir?" asked someone Mirodara assumed to be the warden of the side gate.

"Political prisoner. Escapee. Young girl, thirteen maybe. She has something of value needed by the Consistory."

"We'll keep a watch out for her, sir."

Adarin. Please don't say anything. Please don't say anything.

He didn't. They passed without so much as a peep from the boy. To his credit, he waited until they were well beyond earshot before he crouched down to look for her.

"Well? Can I come down now?"

Mirodara laughed, dropped and rolled out from under the wain. She hopped up and ran away from the merchant caravan. A few surprised merchants reached out to catch her, but she had always been fast. She managed to squeeze past them. She ran down into the deepwood without stopping or looking back.

This part of the Vasylli mountain woods she knew like the back of her hand. Even as a child, her—she almost thought "father," then realized she *had* no father—"treacherous person who raised her" took her often into the woods for days at a time while he would find the best kind of wood for his carpentry. So, finding the backwoods paths that eventually joined the Dar's Way to Nebesta was easy enough.

She ran with inhuman speed all the way to the border of Nebesta. Three days and three nights of nearly constant running and walking, with only short naps for rest whenever she felt like she couldn't go on any more. The rough mountain tracks she followed were well-worn, though strenuous. But she found unexpected reserves of strength inside herself. She ate less than she had expected, and she traveled farther, faster than she had thought possible.

When she joined the Dar's Way, she was sure some sort of alarm would blare the moment she stepped onto the pavement. Nothing happened. At least, nothing she could detect. But there did seem to be some kind of unseen energy that hummed on the level of emotion, just beyond sound. She was unsure if she had caused it, or if it was some devilry of the Raven. It left her stomach queasy. But she resumed her easy pace without any hindrance.

She knew that just before the Way crossed over into Nebesta, it would rise up onto a ridge, then fall away steeply into a shallow valley walled by two tree-covered hills. If there was going to be an ambush anywhere, it would be there. So, she took her time cresting it, listening for the slightest sound of pursuit or ambush. But she heard nothing at all. Not even the sounds of animals. That frightened her, and as she crested the ridge, her breathing became shallow and spots danced before her eyes.

On the downslope, a wall blocked the Dar's Way. It was not very tall yet, clearly in the process of being built, though it was dark and imposing. Menacing, even.

The moment she stopped to stare at the wall, she heard it. Horses behind her.

She ran to the wall and tried to find a handhold to launch herself over into Nebesta and safety, but her hand shot back in pain as though there were tiny barbs all along the wall. She looked at her palm, and it was bloody. Her arm pulsed with pain. Had she just poisoned herself?

She turned around to face whatever it was that was coming after her. Three horsemen. Gumiren. They were bloodied and their eyes were wild and hungry. She would get no quarter from these. They looked like they had just escaped one of the latest pogroms.

"Why you out here, Vasylli girl-child?" asked the central of the three, the youngest.

She said nothing.

He talked to his neighbor in their rat-a-tat tongue. They quickly came to a consensus.

"Your hand." He pointed. "It bloody."

"Yes?" she said. "The wall. It's..."

"Pricked...yes? Keep you in. Keep others out. We guard the wall. All who touch it are for to be executed. You not know this?"

She gulped hard and shook her head. These Gumiren had death in their eyes. She supposed she should be grateful it was only death she saw in their eyes.

"Well, it sad for you. But law is law."

He nodded at the Gumir at his left. In a smooth motion, he pulled a knife from his belt and threw it at Mirodara. It struck her in the chest, the blade going in all the way to the hilt. She stared at it in fascination, before the spots began to dance in her eyes and her knees wobbled. The ground reached up and grabbed her. No, it was the Gumiren. They hoisted her above their heads, she thought. Then, the sensation of weightlessness, followed by the earth falling on her body. No, it was she who fell on the earth. Why was it so hard to concentrate? Everything hurt, especially her left leg. Strange. Why her left leg? She felt at the thing that tugged at her chest. It was knobby. That didn't belong there. She wrenched it out, and a fountain of red poured up and out of her. It was mesmerizing.

Then she realized it was her blood. She seemed to be drowning in it. But no. It wasn't just blood. There was a great deal of water. And it smelled...like...roses.

Voran and Aglaia—he still had trouble thinking of her as Aglaia when she was in her wolf form—had been traveling toward

Vasyllia in a straight line for a week. It was the first time they had done that since the fall of Vasyllia, almost ten years before. At every step, Voran expected that the road would fade, that he would fall into a different realm, or that reality would shift around him, and he would find himself where he had started a week before.

Returning to Vasyllia was impossible. He had tried it. Hundreds of times. But someone—whether Zmei and his brothers or the Raven, Voran didn't know—had made the lands before Vasyllia a warren of hidden doorways and traps. Time and time again, Voran took a step toward Vasyllia, only to find himself in the Lows of Aer, or displaced hundreds of miles farther away from Vasyllia. Something was doing everything in its power to prevent anyone from approaching Vasyllia.

It also didn't help that he hardly had a day when he wasn't running away from Zmei or his giant brothers. It didn't take him long to realize that they had noses like hounds, and they were nearly always three steps ahead of him every time he made his way toward Vasyllia. A few times the encounters had been close to fatal. When his mother Aglaia had joined him in her wolf form, it had actually gotten worse. The giants had bound her to her wolf form in the first place, and somehow her presence made them seek him out ever more ferociously. But she had refused to leave him. She still bristled if he so much as mentioned it.

There were other reasons Voran didn't come back to Vasyllia earlier. One was that Voran had been healing everyone he could find. As Zmei had predicted, the power of the Living Water only lasted for some time. Voran learned to supplement its lack with a thorough study of herbs and medicines from every leech he could find, in whatever village he happened to be at the time. Those travels had taken him as far as Karila, even to the edge of the Steppelands border. He had become a competent enough healer with his hands alone. But sometimes, rarely and never according to his own desire, an echo of the old power came out of his hands, and people were healed by his touch. That alone had been enough to make his legend travel ahead of him. He hoped that it had reached Vasyllia by now.

A year ago, something had happened that made him seek Vasyllia with renewed energy. Lyna stopped coming to him. He realized in the pit of his gut that she was upset with him for not managing to return to Vasyllia. For not accomplishing his calling, so to speak. He felt he had had little choice in the matter, but her lack was like a knife slowly cutting a hole in his chest. He needed her like he needed to breathe. So, he and Aglaia had braved the most obscure paths, some of them nothing more than pure deepwood, with little more than pressed-down grass from the passage of some wild animal.

It took much longer than it normally would. Finding food was a problem, even for Aglaia. But they had done it without even a whiff of giant-stink anywhere near them. Somehow, either the traps had faded in power, or they had managed to evade them. Finally, they came to a sharp ridge of mountains. In them was a narrow pass, hardly noticeable to the naked eye, beyond which lay a hunter's track that connected with the Dar's Way near the border between Nebesta and Vasyllia.

The trek over the pass was difficult—it was late spring, and the cold and ice were omnipresent—but they made it over with only scrapes and bruises, not broken bones. Voran was continually astounded by the unseen grace that protected him in the wild. Sometimes it was just a whisper of a thought that kept him from falling into a crevasse in the night. Sometimes, it was more obvious, like the gust of wind that had actually lifted and carried him and Aglaia over a gap in the mountains that a mountain goat couldn't have jumped. Voran was sure it was no wind, but possibly even a Majestva, one of the higher Powers of Adonais. But he kept his thoughts to himself, and Aglaia had not commented.

Finally, they were within visual range of the border.

A wall towered between Nebesta and Vasyllia, uncommonly high. Higher than the red-barks in Vasyllia, without a doubt.

Voran didn't think human beings could build such things. Perhaps it was the giants?

As usual, it was as though his mother had read his thoughts: "No, that doesn't smell of giants, Voran. Very clearly Raven-made."

"Not Gumiren?"

She sniffed the air for a long time, her head bobbing up and down hypnotically. She did this for more than a minute. Then she huffed and sneezed.

"Some Gumiren. But I think it's an old smell. Very little human smell at all, actually."

They approached it carefully. Voran unsheathed his sword, and Aglaia's hackles rose in concert. Her low growl made the ground shake. It gave Voran the needed push of courage.

Nothing stopped them as they approached, their eyes fixed on the wall. Voran could see no way in or out. He could see precious little at all, as though this were not a wall, but a single, strangely-shaped piece of stone that snaked along the border. It stank of dark magic, even to him. Aglaia's nose wrinkled more and more with distaste the closer they came.

Then, sudden as a sunrise in the middle of winter, the smell. Tube-rose and lavender. Even a hint of orange.

"Is that...?" Aglaia ventured, her tail out straight behind her.

"Yes, it has to be," said Voran. "Only Living Water smells like that."

The road bent leftward, just before rising toward the first ridge of the Vasylli mountains. As they turned the corner, Voran saw the strangest thing he had ever seen. And he had seen some very strange things.

It was a dome-topped square building, similar to the kind of chapel to Adonais that rich merchants liked to build on crossroads in the wild. But it was built entirely of thick vines with vaguely heart-shaped leaves. Tiny purple-blue flowers exploded from the vines at regular intervals. The dome was an interweaving of some fibrous, root-like material that from a distance looked like an oversized onion. It was tipped with a single white blossom with eight petals, larger than any flower he had ever seen.

"What in the Heights...?" Voran said.

"The smell..." said Aglaia, "it's not coming from that edifice. It's from *inside it*."

Voran's hands shook. But it wasn't fear. It was the overawing sense of presence that he used to feel in the Temple in Vasyllia in the old days. A sense he had not had in the wild for many years. It almost physically pushed him down. He felt the need to approach it on his knees.

The vines moved with the slight breeze, revealing a chamber within the strange edifice.

"There's something inside," said Voran, a little lamely.

Aglaia chuckled. "You always become so painfully obvious when you're in the presence of the grace of the Heights."

Voran smiled.

He pushed aside the vines, and a light shone from within— warm and yellow, like a firelight. He climbed in.

A girl lay on a bed of moss and leaves. Her hair—wavy and strawberry blond—reached to her ankles. Her hands were crossed on her chest, where they barely covered a wound from a very wide knife-thrust.

"She's alive! Look at her nails," said Aglaia.

She was right. Her nails were long and curled, as though they had been growing for years.

"But how? That wound would kill a warrior, much less a girl like that."

"I think she's been here for years," said Aglaia, ignoring him. "This place smells strange. Fresh and old at the same time. Only one other place has ever smelled like this. The barrier between the worlds."

Voran reached for the girl's clothes, and realized they were wet through. Her hair remained strangely dry. What sort of place was this?

A compulsion came upon him. He recognized it. It was the same as the push he had felt the night he first heard the Sirin in the forest. He turned the girl over to reach at her back.

She wore a pack made of old canvas, from which the ivy that made the walls grew. This was the source of everything. He opened it gently, and the smell of tuberose inundated him. His hand touched something metal. He pulled it out and gasped.

"That is gorgeous," said Aglaia. She had turned human again, her eyes filling with tears.

The object shimmered in the strange light inside the room. It looked like a budding flower erupting from a nest of leaves. Only it was metal. As he turned it over, he saw that one side was smeared with blood. He tried to wipe it off, but it seemed to have welded to the metal itself. Suddenly, the flask grew heavy in his hand, as though filling with water.

"What in the Heights?" Voran dropped the flask, and it fell down on the girl, overturning its contents of what looked like, and smelled like, Living Water. He picked it up again, and it was once again full.

The girl gasped and sat up, eyes wide.

"I died," she said. "You brought me back." She looked at Voran, then at the flask. "I think I understand."

"I don't," said Voran, crouching down to the girl, examining her chest to see that there was nothing, not even a scratch, left from a wound that was surely fatal.

"A final gift," she said, her voice not quite her own. "for the Healer. It is the final sacrifice of Llun the smith for the sake of the reclamation of Vasyllia."

A song like wind whistling through reeds sounded all around them. Lyna the Sirin showered them with her song. The ivy burst apart in flames that were warm, but not burning. The sun streamed down on them, far too warm for this time of year. The girl's eyes opened wide and she laughed.

"You are real!" she said. "The Sirin. You are real!"

"You came back," said Voran, his voice shaking with the joy-pierced sorrow that he had not sensed for what seemed an eternity. "Thank you. I can breathe again."

"Yes, my Voran. I come to confirm this blessing. But it is one laden with pain."

"Is it ever not, Lyna?" Voran laughed ruefully.

"This flask contains Living Water. An inexhaustible source. But it will only remain as long as the Healer heals. If you leave your path, your chosen calling, it will empty and not fill again. And your path does not lead to Vasyllia. Not yet."

And so, Voran walked away from the wall, away from Vasyllia, away from his beloved Sabíana. His heart was a stone inside him, the flask was a burden on his hip. He turned back to the wall a final time.

When will I see you again, my Sabíana? Voran thought.

The girl stopped next to him, staring up at him with eyes that had not yet returned to the mundane.

"What will you do now?" she asked.

"I will do what I'm supposed to do," he said. "Ready the rest of the lands for the return of Vasyllia. Stop the internecine war that's raging among the city-states. Prepare the soil of people's hearts for the bond-fire of the Sirin."

"You will do all that? You're only one man."

He laughed bitterly. "Sometimes, there is only one man left who is willing to do what must be done." He sighed. "Where will you go, little thing?"

Her expression clouded, like she was trying to remember something important.

"She's coming with me," said Aglaia. "We're going to find her a place to rest and heal. Maybe Nebesta, maybe farther away."

"So, you're finally letting me out on my own?" he asked, smiling.

The wolf sniffed loudly through her nose. "You have to grow up someday. Might as well be today."

Did you enjoy this book? You can make a big difference!

Review are the most powerful tools that I have when it comes to getting attention to my books. Although I'm not a starving artist, I don't have the financial muscle to take out full page ads in the *New York Times*.

But I do have something more powerful than that.

A committed, excited, and loyal group of readers.

If you've enjoyed my novel, I would be very grateful if you'd spend only five minutes to leave a short review on any book retail page and Goodreads.

Thank you very much! And be sure to read the exclusive preview of book 3 in the series on the next page.

Chapter 1: Khaidu

Khaidu had not always wished for death. She still remembered when the sky's endless abyss spoke to her in hushed tones. She used to prance like a goat on the mountains while her ten brothers laughed at her. Now that she couldn't walk, now that her face was a broken ruin, now that she could hardly speak two words without the pain in her head turning white-hot, they no longer laughed at all. Not in her presence.

Her family, the last true nomads of the Gumiren, had a saying. *The Steppe is a hard mother.* The Steppe provided food and grass for the herds. The Steppe gave water and firm land, comfortable for the feet of the horses. The Steppe's endless sky and limitless grass—it was a home as great as the earth itself. But the Steppe was cold. The Steppe was wind and driving snow. The Steppe was dearth and labor and, sometimes, death.

Khaidu often wished her hard mother, the Steppe, would end her.

"You need something to distract you, my little wolfling," said Etchigu one day as he came into her yurt with two steaming cups of salty tea. He was the only brother who still spoke to Khaidu. She suspected that he did it only because it was his duty as eldest.

"I've spoken to Mamai," he continued. "She is willing, this once, to let you come on the hunt."

Khaidu laughed, though through her crooked mouth it sounded more like hissing. She made the sign that meant "horses will fly before that day comes."

Etchigu smiled. "Yes, I know it isn't proper for a girl to come. But Mamai can make an exception."

"Hhhoold...f-f-fasttt."

"To tradition? Yes, we must. You needn't remind me. I know we're all that's left of the Gumiren in the Steppe. But you need this, little one. And I know you want it."

"Y-y-yes…" A little ember of delight lit up somewhere deep inside her.

A rumbling sound, like the soft growl of a bear, rose up outside the yurt. It was echoed by the rhythmic strumming on a three-string *tobashur*. Then someone started to play the bowed two-string *kabukar*. To Khaidu, it sounded like a river breaking free of ice in spring. Her ember of delight flared into the beginning of joy.

Etchigu must have caught her expression, because his eyes lit up with more than the light of her dim hearth-fire.

"Yes," he said. "I asked the boys to sing the one about the wolf cub who couldn't hunt."

"D-d-did…y-y-ou…hm-hm-hm…" She was too tired to go on, but Etchigu caught her drift.

"Yes, I asked them to sing it in 'mother bear.'"

It was Khaidu's favorite. There were three kinds of overtone singing, some more piercing than others. But the rumble of the mother-bear—it had a quality that sweetened even the worst pain for Khaidu, though it was laced with wistfulness and loss.

Etchigu carried her out of the yurt. Four of her brothers sat around a large fire. Three of them were playing their homemade *tobashuri* and *kabukar*, and the fourth was searching for the overtone, his eyes closed. All the muscles of his face were slack, except for his eyebrows, which threatened to bore into the bones of his head, they were so tight. Then they relaxed, and the overtone poured out just as the logs of the fire cracked and fell in on each other. A shower of sparks rose, then faded into the heavy fog encircling them.

As soon as the singing started, children materialized out of the fog. The evening song called to them, and they were always preternaturally quiet when "mother bear" was used. It soothed Khaidu, for whom their physical games were a constant reminder of her loss. Then one of them, probably some distant cousin of Khaidu's that she could never remember—there were so many of them, after all—moved into a dancing-pattern that mirrored the words of the song.

"A cub there was, who howled with hunger ...

All the faces turned toward the fire were calm, but smiling. This was *right*. At such moments, the painful reality of being a people in exile faded into the larger tapestry of their Gumiren history—so rich, so ancient, and so pure. At least until the recent time of darkness.

"Her legs were weak; her teeth were cracked ..."

A masked figure with trailing sleeves of bright red emerged from the darkness. Khaidu's heart leaped. It was a rare thing for the old shaman's daughter, a dancer of the spirits, to come out for the evening song, to transform it into more than a simple remembrance. Her movements, inspired by mystical currents in the eternal expanse of the sky, gathered all the threads of their individual worries, desires, aspirations, and intertwined them into a single petition to the silence of the Heights. To the Unknown Father whom all true Gumiren have sought for hundreds, perhaps thousands, of years.

"Many were the years of hunger, many the days of pain..."

The spirit-dancer spun on one foot, then seemed to fall, until she caught herself at the final moment. It looked as though someone had lifted her by an invisible string attached at her shoulder. Back and forth she swayed, softly humming along as her fingers, arms, and legs painted pictures that spoke in a silent language of supplication.

Until she shed her downy fur and tasted her first kill..."

Khaidu's eyes hurt from the firelight. She closed them. With something like surprise, she felt wet drops fall on her hands, lying upturned on legs like matchsticks. Was she crying?

Will I ever shed my downy fur? she wondered. Then the bitterness rose up again. *No. More likely I will be the first kill, not taste it...*

Three days later came the Red Day, named for the unbearable fire of the first sunset of spring. It was the first wolf-hunt of the year, fraught with special significance. In the misty morning, all the hunters bantered, eager for the start of the hunting season. They fell silent as Etchigu carried Khaidu out of her yurt. He strapped her into the special saddle designed for her lifeless legs and too-strong arms. The silence grew to murmurs, all of them unfriendly. Khaidu heard them all:

"What is Etchigu doing? This is not allowed..."

"A bad omen, especially for Red Day..."

"Has Mamai gone soft in the head?"

Only Batuk (Khaidu's personal torturer) had the courage to walk up to Etchigu and openly remonstrate. Etchigu took him aside and spoke in angry whispers. Khaidu tried not to listen, but she heard enough.

"How much longer does she have? Have some pity," whispered Etchigu. That was especially painful to hear, but it seemed to work. Batuk subsided, though the look he gave Khaidu promised no respite from future pain.

Khaidu tried not to care, though the tears were already threatening to come. Not an auspicious beginning for the hunt.

It took them most of the day to approach the hunting fields. As they rode, the beauty of the landscape pushed aside all Khaidu's other thoughts. This Red Day seemed created by the Powers especially for her. As the sun set, the horse-clan's hunters —twenty picked men, ten of whom were Khaidu's brothers— stilled their horses on the tips of the Teeth, the last ridges before the mountain flowed wave-like down into the Steppe. The setting sun gilded their furry-eared hats and the plumed heads of their hunting eagles. They stood in a rough semicircle, each hunter the prescribed ten paces away from his neighbor, just close enough to hear the raised voice of the hunt leader. The horses stamped and tossed their heads in frustration, their breath clouding around them. The eagles shrugged—first one shoulder, then another—anxious to begin. Khaidu thought her heart would explode from the beauty of it all.

Yeeeeeeaaaaaaaaaaaauuuuuuuuuuuuu!!!

Khaidu's heart caught in her throat at the sound of Etchigu's hunt shriek. The horses flew over the lip of the Teeth, and their breath mingled with the fresh powder thrown up by eighty hooves in concert. Etchigu launched into an old ballad, and Batuk backed him, adding his own improvised harmony to Etchigu's raspy tenor. Then all the men joined in, and the river of song grew to a torrent. For a moment, Khaidu thought the eagles sang with them as well, their wings half-unfurled, their darting tongues visible in their open beaks.

The single wolf in the valley below looked up, as though curious. Arelat, Etchigu's eagle, screamed. At that sound, the wolf turned and fled. The sons of Mamai jani-Beg, the greatest matriarch of the Gumiren, shouted the final chord of the ballad and threw their arms up. Gold-flecked in the evening light, the eagles leaped up, awkwardly catching the air as though they were out of practice. All together as one, they caught a thermal and spun around each other, dancing, then each wheeled out and plunged down toward the fleeing wolf. For a moment, Khaidu felt a pang for the poor creature. No wolf, no matter how big, could come away unscathed from a Gumiren eagle attack.

Suddenly, Arelat the eagle banked left, nearly crashing into the other eagles in mid-air. Khaidu forgot to breathe in surprised shock. An eagle twice the size of Arelat materialized seemingly out of nowhere. It was black as a raven, except for the head and tail, which were whiter than new snow. Incensed at the challenge, Arelat dove at the intruder. At the last possible moment, the great white-headed beast maneuvered out of the way. Arelat missed.

Khaidu gasped. This could be the end of Arelat as chief hunter's eagle.

But the white-headed monster seemed to have no interest in

dominating the rest of the eagles. Its behavior was unlike anything Khaidu had ever seen. It wheeled back and forth, toward the other eagles, then toward the riders, then back up into the expanse of sky, seemingly for the joy of flight alone.

Khaidu slowed her horse to a complete stop. The black and white eagle compelled her with a yearning stronger than thought. She wanted the eagle for herself, to bind it to herself as all hunting eagles were bound to Gumiren hunters. She wanted to show them all she was worth something. No, it was more than that. She ached to have her own purpose within the rule-bound world of the Gumiren nomads, the world that had no place for a cripple.

Etchigu had taught her the song of binding; would her body cooperate?

Khaidu raised her gloved right hand, palm up, toward the eagle. She keened that peculiar call that so enticed all eagles. The inside of her head convulsed with pain. The eagle shuddered and stopped in mid-soar. Her tongue cramped and her throat burned with the effort, but Khaidu gritted her teeth and kept on. She wrapped her awkward lips around the words of the binding.

The eagle trembled, battling with what Khaidu could only imagine was an ecstasy like nothing a human being could bear. It broke free for a moment and managed to fly up a few feet, then again seemed chained in place, shuddering in midair. The other eagles circled it now, and Arelat was primed to strike at the now helpless creature.

Now, thought Khaidu. *To me!*

The eagle plunged toward her, and the rest of the eagles followed in single file like the tail of a spirit-banner snapping in wind. Khaidu focused her song to a higher pitch, then reached deep within her throat to find the elusive overtone. When she found it, the sound pushed through her broken body like a spear-thrust, and she almost lost the thread of the music in the ecstasy that erased all her pain. That was the final blow. The eagle veered, then alighted clumsily on Khaidu's gloved hand. Khaidu fell silent, and the eagle remained in place. It worked.

Up close, she saw that it was not quite twice the size of a normal Steppe-eagle, but even with her strong arms, Khaidu had to strain to keep it steady. It looked at her with eyes nearly human and clicked its beak. For a terrifying moment, Khaidu thought it would peck her eyes out. Then it squawked and preened like a sparrow.

With her other hand, Khaidu grasped the thick mane of her pony and whistled. The pony cantered down toward the ragged line of hunters who had stopped in the middle of the slope. They all looked at her as though she had grown a second head. She smiled internally. Far away, barely more than a speck of dust, the grey wolf ran like the wind. If wolves could speak, he would have a story to tell that would make him a legend. The only wolf ever to escape a Gumiren hunt.

Etchigu clicked his tongue, and his horse pushed uphill toward Khaidu. He smiled broadly, his eyes lost in the folds above his high cheekbones.

"Well, well, wolfling," he said. "Trying to take my place as head hunter?" His laugh was raspy—a sure sign of real enjoyment. He regarded the eagle, the whites of his eyes stark against the winter-burn red of his face. "What a beast! Poor Arelat. He'll never live it down."

Khaidu gathered every ounce of physical strength left to speak. "Gh..hh...ank you....f-f-for t-t-take...mmme."

"You're welcome," he said. He raised his arm and whistled. Arelat came, but with bowed head. It avoided looking at Khaidu. Her eagle completely ignored Arelat, intent on Khaidu's face. She felt the heat of the gaze, as if it were human. It gave her a perverse kind of enjoyment. But the best was the embarrassment on Batuk's face.

~

The hunting party's return journey was interminable. Eagle, pony, and hunter alike rode with heads half-bowed. Khaidu alone rejoiced as she contemplated her eagle circling overhead, never too far away from its new master. Lost in her thoughts, Khaidu did not realize that she had fallen behind the rest, with only Batuk still behind her. Panic pushed out joy in an instant.

Batuk trotted up to her. Etchigu was too far for her to cry out. She willed her pony to canter. She was too late. Batuk rode alongside, matching her pace. His eyes were like two prods on her left cheek. I will not panic, she said to herself. Her heart refused to listen. Already the cramping in her hands presaged one of her fits. Batuk did it on purpose. He wanted her to have a fit and fall off. She was so far behind the rest that it would take a long time for anyone to realize that something was amiss.

She knew what she had to do. "Breathe long, extend your fingers, turn the rocks in your neck into water," said Mamai's voice in her head, but Khaidu only felt herself curling inward like a poppy closing at night.

"You shouldn't have come," said Batuk, wolfish. "You ruined the hunt for us."

It seemed Batuk was not content with waiting for her fit. He struck her on the back of the head, in the place that hurt more than any other, as he knew well enough. A light flashed behind her eyes, a moan bubbled up from deep inside her, and she fell to the ground, screaming like an animal being butchered.

But no. That was not her screaming. Batuk screamed. The white-headed eagle was on top of him, scraping his face with its talons. Even in the tangle of hands and black feathers, the telltale red splashed.

The rest of the party rushed back, but they were far away. By the time they arrived, Batuk's face was a ruin.

Khaidu retched on the ground, barely managing to avoid fouling herself with the sickness. Her body throbbed with pain, her mouth was fuzzy and tasted of metal. With an effort, she moved her tongue over the inside of her cheek—it was thick as felt and ragged. She suspected she had bitten though her tongue. Something sharp and insistent pounded at her left hip. She sobbed. To her own ears, she sounded like little more than a wounded animal. Something reptilian and repulsive, worse than a lamed horse or a sick dog.

Etchigu picked her up. His expression was difficult to read.

"Khaidu, did Batuk attack you?" he asked quietly.

She shook all over but managed to force her head up and down. Etchigu sighed.

"Then he deserved what he got. But Mamai will be furious. There's something you must understand, little wolf. You are responsible for that eagle now. If it attacks anyone else, you will have to put it down. You do not know the pain of killing your own eagle. It is worse than losing a prize stallion."

The hunters stopped soon afterward, warding the four corners of their makeshift camp with the ragged spirit-banners. The pain from her fit was now a dull throb. Etchigu helped her set up a stoop for her eagle inside her travel tent, as was traditional for a full-fledged hunter. Khaidu nearly burst with pride, looking at her eagle. But the eagle ignored her, staring into space for a long time, still as a statue. Khaidu fell asleep.

She woke up to someone shaking her hard. A woman. In panic, Khaidu looked at the stoop. It was empty.

"What have you done to my—?" Khaidu cried out but was struck dumb at the sight of the woman.

She was dark-haired, slim, her skin the color of olive-meat, reddening at the cheeks. But it was her dress that stopped Khaidu—heavy wine-red brocade embroidered with gold suns and moons—a dress of greater worth than the entire horse-clan of Mamai jani-Beg.

"What have you done to me?" the woman said. "Who are you? Are you a wielder of power?"

"I don't know what you—?" Khaidu fell silent. She was talking. Like a normal person.

Khaidu looked down at herself, and her legs were rounded with muscle. They moved when she willed them to. With trembling hands, she traced the too-familiar path of the scars running down her face, but they were gone. Her face was whole, intact, symmetrical. The drooping, scarred half was as firm as a ripe pear. She was herself again.

"I am Sabíana, Darina of the Vasylli," whispered the woman fiercely. "I am also, as you so rudely suggested, *your* eagle. I demand that you tell me who you are, and how you bound me to yourself."

The Heart of the World is available in all formats at your local in person or online retailer

ABOUT THE AUTHOR

Nicholas Kotar is a writer of epic fantasy inspired by Russian fairy tales, a freelance translator from Russian to English, the resident conductor of the men's choir at a Russian monastery in the middle of nowhere, and a semi-professional vocalist. His one great regret in life is that he was not born in the nineteenth century in St. Petersburg, but he is doing everything he can to remedy that error.

ALSO BY NICHOLAS KOTAR

The Raven Son Series:
The Song of the Sirin
The Curse of the Raven
The Heart of the World
The Forge of the Covenant
The Throne of the Gods

The Worldbuilding Series:
How to Survive a Russian Fairy Tale
Heroes for All Time
A Window to the Russian Soul

Russian Fairy Tales and Myths:
In a Certain Kingdom: Fairy Tales of Old Russia

Made in the USA
Monee, IL
05 January 2023

24425108R00062